Richard Johnson

Moral Sketches for Young Minds

Richard Johnson

Moral Sketches for Young Minds

ISBN/EAN: 9783337011956

Printed in Europe, USA, Canada, Australia, Japan

Cover: Foto ©Andreas Hilbeck / pixelio.de

More available books at **www.hansebooks.com**

MORAL SKETCHES

FOR

YOUNG MINDS.

───────────

And when the clofing Scenes prevail,
When Wealth, State, Pleafure, All fhall fail;
All that a foolifh World admires,
Or Paffion craves, or Pride infpires;
At that important Hour of Need,
Virtue fhall prove a Friend indeed!

───────────

LONDON:

Printed for E. NEWBERY, the Corner of
St. Paul's Church Yard,

1797.
[Price One Shilling.]

ADVERTISEMENT.

IF a Work folely intended to promote Virtue and Morality, to arm the rifing Generation againſt the prevailing Follies of the Age, and to point out to them thoſe Objects which muſt regulate their Welfare here and hereafter, be worthy of the Patronage of good Parents, Friends, and Guardians of Children, then theſe Moral Sketches have little to fear on account of the. Reception they will meet with.

This Work contains a great Variety of ſhort Eſſays, on moſt

A 2   of

of the moral Duties of Life, and were originally written in French by a Pen, which Death has long since silenced. If the Translator of these invaluable Sketches shall be thought to have sent them into the World in an easy and elegant English dress, he aspires to no other Fame. May every youthful Mind receive as much Instruction and Advantage from the Perusal of them, as the Translator felt Pleasure in naturalizing them into the English Language.

MORAL.

MORAL SKETCHES.

FRIENDSHIP.

IT is faid, that the fcarcity of any thing encreafes its value, and that gold and filver for that reafon hold the firft place among perifhable matters; yet it muft be confeffed, that there is one thing in this world more fcarce than thofe metals, and that is, a true friend, if fuch a thing be at all poffible to be found. There is perhaps too much reafon to believe, that though almoft every one talks of a Friend and a Phœnix, no perfon has ever yet feen either.

As for fafhionable friends, thefe are every day to be met with; but they are like flies that crowd round a honey-pot, only to rob it of its fweets. Such friends are generally found to refemble fwallows, who vifit us in the fpring to enjoy the
approaching

approaching warmth of the fummer, and quit us as foon as the winter commences. There are few friends who love us equally with themfelves, and who will prefer our intereft to their own. Men form thofe connections, which are often diftinguifhed by the name of friendfhip, either out of intereft, for the fake of converfation, and often merely as companions of favourite vices. Daily experience convinces us, that as foon as fortune forfakes us, our friends turn their backs on us, find no more pleafure in our converfation, and we become unworthy of even being a partner in their vices.

Dionyfius the Tyrant, wanting one day to fpeak with the Prince, his fon, fent to him to defire him to come and fup with him. The young Prince, being feated at table when he received the meffage, begged to be excufed, and affured the meffenger, that he would pay his refpects to his father as foon as he had finifhed his fupper, and accordingly fulfilled his promife on rifing from the table.

When

When the Prince approached his father, the Tyrant afked him, why he did not come and fup with him? " Becaufe (faid the Prince) I had five or fix friends at my table." Dionyfius appeared to be furprifed at his fon's having fo many friends, and afked him if he were fully perfuaded of their friendfhip? to which the Prince replied, that he had not the leaft doubt of their fincerity.

" Their friendfhip then (faid the father) muft be put to the trial, and, for that purpofe, order them all to attend you this night in your own apartment. Make them your confidants, and tell them, that you have affaffinated the Tyrant, and beg of them to affift you in removing the body, and burying it privately, in order that his death may be kept a fecret, till the minds of the people fhall be prevailed on to place you on the throne in the room of your father. After having thus experienced their fidelity, come and give me an account of it, that you and I may rejoice together

on

on the ineftimable treafure you have found in fo many friends."

The young Prince executed the orders of the Tyrant, and put the fincerity of his friends to that delicate proof; but how great was his furprife when he found, that of all thofe, who, while at fupper, with full glaffes in hand, protefted they would cheerfully die to ferve him, not one now offered to engage in fo perilous an undertaking, and each ftole away one after the other!

The Prince acquainted the Tyrant with the ill fuccefs of his experiment, when his father wifely faid to him : " My fon, for the future, take care in whom you place your confidence. Be affured, that there are few men fo happy in this world, as, in the courfe of their whole lives, to find *one* fincere friend ; and that the friends of the table, as foon as the repaft is finifhed, often fecretly defpife their benefactor."

JOY.

JOY.

JOY is generally a proof of the contentment of the heart, and is usually the companion of a good conscience. Hence people of a lively difposition are generally preferred to thofe of an auftere, dull, and gloomy caft, whofe four and formal converfation contributes only to infpire wearinefs and difguft.

I remember, when I was a child, that I took notice of people, who I was told were learned, and who generally appeared to me of fo melancholy and gloomy a temper, that they infpired me with a kind of averfion for ftudy. It is not that I expect extravagant joy, which is accompanied with perpetual peals of laughter, and which pleafes by chattering like a parrot, jumping about like a magpie, and doing fuch things as border upon madnefs; but I am a friend to that gaiety of difpofition, which is confined within the bounds of decency, which fhews us contented with ourfelves and others, which fpreads
a ferene

a ferene and pleafing air over the countenance, and which from time to time
produces thofe little fparks of wit that
occafion moderate laughter, leaving others
an opportunity to make us laugh in their
turn.   I cannot endure thofe fevere people,
who, under the veil of gravity, wifh to
impofe on the world, and who cannot fuffer
any other difcourfes than politics, morality,
or philofophy, without mixing with them
the leaft fentiment of mirth, or any little
piece of hiftory to amufe us.

Joy is an antidote to melancholy and
chagrin, and often gives eafe to the infirmities of the body ; it enlivens the fpirits,
and mocks the caprice of fortune; it calms
the ftorm of difgrace, makes us fenfible to
the pleafures of life, and contributes to
prolong our exiftence here.

SORROW.

IF we contemplate the affairs of this
world with an eye of philofophy, we fhall
find nothing worthy of either our joy or
forrow.   The one, however, appears more
reafonable

reasonable than the other. Joy promotes the health of the body; but Sorrow confumes mankind as the fire does wax.

Sorrow is the confequence of difgrace, and that often fprings from the imagination, which being generally a falfe reprefenter of objects, and our ideas being often hurried away by felf-love, we are led to confider our forrows as grievous, when, in reality, they are founded only in weaknefs. Since then, every thing which we fee, poffefs, love, hate, feek, or fhun, in this world, is fubject to annihilation, and fince every thing which nature has mafqued under fome form or figure, muft in the end be reduced to nothing, why fhould we make ourfelves wretched at the lofs of that nothing?

Men are fometimes driven to defpair on the lofs of their worldly poffeffions, without reflecting, that they brought nothing with them into the world, and can carry nothing out of it. Others fhew an immoderate grief on the lofs of a friend or a parent, without reflecting, that man is nothing
but

but an earthly walking machine, and cannot always exift; but according to the courfe of all earthly beings, muft at laft return to duft: fo that thofe who die only go a few days before thofe they leave behind them.

A third perfon weeps to-day for his extreme indigence, who perhaps to morrow may be in want of nothing. A fourth is ready to burft with grief, on hearing his reputation wounded by the falfe tongue of fcandal, and builds his wretchednefs on empty founds, that were loft in the air, and could exift only for a few moments. In fpeaking of Sorrow, I recollect the wife manner in which a fage confoled Queen Arfinoe, and which Plutarch relates nearly in the following words.

" When Jupiter diftributed among his infernal fpirits the different offices of his gloomy empire, Sorrow, who is one of thofe evil fpirits, came to folicit a place, but was a little too late, as he had already difpofed of the principal places in the kingdom of the dead. Among the employments

ployments which yet remained to be diſtributed, the maſter of the gods made his diviſion of the Tears, Sighs, Regrets, and all the ſentiments, which the loſs of a dear friend inſpires, and placed Sorrow at the head of them; but as neither of theſe infernal ſpirits ever ſtay long but with thoſe who receive them kindly, ſo Sorrow never takes up its abode, but where the Tears, Sighs, and Chagrin, have made a previous poſſeſſion.

" This diſcourſe appeared ſo reaſonable to Arſinoë, that from that moment ſhe diſmiſſed her Sorrow, and endeavoured to conſole herſelf. Thus thoſe, who do not wiſh prematurely to quit this world, muſt baniſh frightful ſorrow from their boſoms, and meet the calamities of this life with heroic fortitude, wiſely reflecting, that ſince the ſmiles or the frowns of fortune muſt one day have an end, neither of them ought to give us too much concern."

B   *CHANCE.*

CHANCE.

CHANCE is the prime minister of Fortune, and executes whatever that blind divinity decrees with respect to mortals. It flies as swift as thought, and comes as unexpectedly as the thief by night. It sometimes suddenly raises us to honours, for which we should have never presumed to hope; and at other times hurls us, from the summit of prosperity, into the gulf of irrecoverable ruin. It sometimes suddenly presents occasions, which according to the use we make of them, decide our happiness or misery for the rest of our lives.

We may venture to say, that unless we have the protection of Divine Providence, which often so miraculously interferes in our favour, that the life of man is composed of chance events, which accompany him from the cradle to the tomb, and which, like favourable or contrary winds, fill the sails of good and bad fortune, and force him forward, according to their caprice,

caprice, into the ports of Profperity, or force him on the rocks of Difgrace, where he inevitably perifhes. Both ancient and modern hiftory afford us many examples of the uncertainty of every poffeffion in this life.

Depreffion of the Mind.

THE Depreffion of the mind, though natural to fome people, is generally the confequence of indolence and idlenefs, and therefore unbecoming in a man. When we employ ourfelves about fomething that is ufeful, we have not leifure to give way to this ftrange difpofition of the mind, and when we properly fill up our time, we fhall always find ourfelves the better fatisfied with our own conduct. Indolence is what nature never defigned for man, but is an invention of his own to torment himfelf.—It is an enemy, which the wife man fhuns, and the fool courts. Animals are ignorant of it, becaufe inftinct never teaches it; and man only pines in imaginary languor, becaufe he has the liberty

of

of fo doing. However, terrible as this diforder may be, every one has the remedy within his own reach; and he who procures a livelihood by induftry in the moft humiliating fituation, is preferable to the monarch, who paffes his wretched hours in rolling about on the couch of indolence, and leaves his duty to be performed by others.

Nature applies herfelf to unremitting labour, and never ftops for a moment, but is perpetually at work to promote and fopport her grand and magnificent operations: while man often fuffers imaginary evils to deprefs his mind, and gives way to indolence, rather than exert himfelf in fome ufeful and profitable employment, which would not fail to cure his diforder, and make him cheerful and happy.

Oreftes often complained of the wretched depreffion and indolence of his mind, and on a friend once advifing him, as an infallible remedy, to roufe himfelf from his lethargy, and apply his time to fome ufeful employment, he replied: " Since
there

there is no better method of being revenged
on time, which deftroys every thing, I
am determined to let it pafs in doing nothing." Such an idea is unworthy of a
human being, and I hope will be confidered as fuch by all my readers, whether
young or aged.

ANGER.

A CERTAIN Philofopher has faid,
" Though the rage of anger is but a
fpecies of madnefs of no long duration, it
often leaves behind it, in its effects, evils
of a lafting nature." It is certain, that
the violent emotion it occafions is one of
the principal obftacles to the tranquility
of life, and the health of the body, fince
it ftifles the judgment and blinds the reafon. A few words dropped in a fit of
anger, often make a man mifcrable all
the reft of his life, fince he may thereby
lofe thofe friends in a few minutes, whom
he had been many years in acquiring.
Befides, that it often difcovers the moft
latent fecrets of the heart, it frequently

renders the paffionate man ridiculous by the threats he utters, which he cannot have in his power to put into execution. How many perfons have paffed the reft of their lives in ufelefs forrow and remorfe for having fuffered themfelves, only for a few moments, to be hurried away by the violence of their paffion !

The friendfhip of a man who gives way to anger, is an incumbrance to fenfible people ; and his company is a labyrinth, into which we more eafily entered, than we can find our way out of it. This is the partition which divides anger from fury, and the paffionate man and the maniac have equally the fame right to a houfe of confinement.

Paffion deprives a man of the ufe of his fenfes, and fo effectually dazzles his fight, that he does not fee the danger into which he is often headlong advancing. It clofes his ears, fo that he cannot hear reafon, and makes him utter words, which, while they can be of no fervice

to

to him, may be productive of a lasting injury.

Hiftory tells us of a man at a certain court, remarkable for the violence of his paffion, who had the infolence to draw his fword in the prefence of his king, and who, after having broken it, threw it at the feet of his fovereign, fwearing he would never ufe it more in the fervice of fuch a king. It is true, that his fovereign fmiled at the extreme folly of his fubject, but he prefently afterwards deprived him of all his lucrative and honourable employments, and fent him to a loathfome prifon, where he had time to lament his folly during fourteen years, when death put a period to his woes.

The paffionate man every moment gives an opportunity to thofe who wifh to injure him; and when a man has conceived a hatred againft another, and the object of his hatred is violent and paffionate, the ruin of the latter is eafily accomplifhed. Of all the feven mortal firs, that of paffion is the greateft diburber of
human

human fociety, and that which affords the finner no pleafure. Thus paffion ferves only to offend God, to ruin the health, and to deprive us of friends and fortune.

LYING.

A LYAR is the object of univerfal contempt and hatred; for, as a lyar is diametrically oppofite to good faith, he muft confequently be a very indignant creature. His tongue is the trumpet of falfehood, and his words are witneffes againft his pretenfions to the title of a man. He never opens his mouth but to his own confufion, and all his fpeeches contribute to difcover his fhame, until he becomes as contemptible in the eyes of honeft men, as he is odious to the Supreme Being. The hatred and contempt of mankind are at laft the rewards of the pains he has taken to fpread falfe reports among his friends. The world, who generally judge wrong on moft other occafions, is not fo with regard to the

lyar,

lyar, but agree with one voice to cenfure and defpife his conduct. It is in vain that he employs oaths to make himfelf believed by thofe to whom he fpeaks; for even truth is difcredited when it comes from his mouth.

The mean and indignant idea of a lyar cannot be made better appear, than by putting it in oppofition to that lively refentment, which every man of honour feels himfelf obliged to fhew when accufed of a lye; he prefers death to fuch an accufation, and freely hazards his life to wipe off fo foul a ftain on his character. The Roman hiftory furnifhes us with ftriking examples of the attachment thofe mafters of the world had to truth. We fhall content ourfelves with relating one inftance, which will be fufficient to fhew how great was their efteem for truth.

When Auguftus, after the defeat of Marc Anthony and Cleopatra, entered Rome in triumph, among the prifoners who followed in his train was an Egyptian prieft, of whom fame faid he had never

told

told a lye in his life. So extraordinary
a character drew on him the attention of.
all the city, and afterwards was rumoured
in the senate; when that illustrious body
thought it their duty to do honour to
truth, though found in the person of a
slave. They ordered him to be presented
with his freedom, and, as he was a priest,
that he should be admitted among those
whose business it was to prepare and make
the sacrifices to the Gods. Lastly, to
do honour to the reign of Augustus, in
which so singular a man was discovered,
they erected statues to this virtuous Egyptian, that posterity might be acquainted
with this event.

Having thus mentioned what distin-
guished honours the Romans conferred
on truth, it is but just that we should
give a striking proof of the indignation
they shewed to a lye. In the reign of
the Emperor Claudius, a man died at
Rome, of whom it was publicly said,
that he had never spoken a word of truth
in his life. The emperor being informed

of

of this, gave orders that the dead body of this notorious lyar fhould be denied all funeral rites, that his houfe fhould be razed to the ground, his poffeffions confifcated, and all his family banifhed for ever, in order entirely to annihilate the memory of fo wicked a man.

Hannibal, though he was the greateft captain of the times in which he lived, was never able to attract the efteem of the people of honour, who were his contemporaries, for having broken his word whenever he found it to his advantage.—Titus Livius fays, that the praifes we cannot refufe to his penetration in council, to his diligence in executing every thing neceffary, and to his intrepidity in battle, were among the number of thofe accomplifhments, which, in this iuftance, we are obliged to allow to a wicked man favoured by fortune.

BENEFICENCE.

AN elevated foul feels nothing more fenfibly, than the pleafure it receives in

in relieving the unfortunate; whereas the
oppofite principle, that of a mean and
fordid foul, feels itfelf hurt in the welfare of another. The noble ambition,
which gives to the firft as many fubjects
of pleafure, as there are unfortunate perfons to be relieved, cannot but be accep-
table to God; but the envy, which the
latter conceives at the profperity of another, is a vice peculiar to the infernal
fpirit.

We cannot nearer approach to the
grand model of perfection which is pro-
pofed to us, than by employing ourfelves
in doing all the good we can to our
fellow-creatures; for it is by thofe means
we are enabled to refemble, in fome meafure, our Father who is in Heaven,
who, without partial regard, caufes the
fun to fhine alike on all. If the condition of the rich and powerful be worthy
of envy, it can be only becaufe they
have it in their power to relieve the
wretched, and fupport thofe who are
finking under the load of misfortune.

                                    Benevolence,

Benevolence, added to power, is furely one of the greateft gifts Heaven has to beftow!

Great and good actions are to the foul as food is to the body; and the beneficence we fhew to others during this life, are certain pledges of thofe which God has promifed in Heaven to the humane and charitable. Thefe amiable virtues pafs not unrewarded even in this world, fince they draw on us the admiration, refpect, and love of mankind, and fecure to our memory the fame honours from pofterity.

I remember to have read part of an epitaph, which agrees with my prefent fubject, and is thus expreffed: "What I have fpent, I have loft; what wealth I poffeffed, I have left to others; but what I gave is ftill my own."

It is certain, that the advantages we derive from the expences of our table or pleafures, are of no longer duration than the fatisfaction they procure, and that is but momentary. Death ftrips us of all our poffeffions, and gives perhaps to ftrangers all our wealth we enjoyed in this world; but our beneficence, which we extend to thofe who ftand in need of it, are treafures, which even God lays up in ftore for us, and which he promifes to reftore to us an hundred fold, when all our other poffeffions fhall have taken wings and fled away. The interefts we derive from our beneficence in this world, are the prayers and bleffings of thofe we have relieved, who inceffantly offer up their beft wifhes to Heaven for our happinefs here and hereafter. The pleafure of good actions affords us comfort in our paffage through life, and fupports us in the expiring moments of our exiftence.

LAUGHTER.

LAUGHTER is a quality peculiar to man alone, nature not having endowed any other creature with the power of contracting their features into fuch forms.

Laughter

Laughter is the enfign of joy, and frequently the trumpet of folly.

To laugh on every occafion, is a proof that we are agreeably furprized at the view of every trifle that prefents itfelf, and confequently betrays a fimple genius, and the want of difcernment. A man, who laughs much, in the end makes himfelf ridiculous; and the woman, who has this defect, is truely to be pitied; for, befides that modefty, which is the real ornament of their fex, fuffers much from it, excefs of laughter disfigures the countenance, enlarges the mouth, and fwells the cheeks; fo that, by giving too much way to this folly, a lovely countenance may be changed into the mafk of a fool. It is true, that the dimpled fmile is an additional beauty to a fine face, but it muft not be accompanied with an unnatural extenfion of the voice.

It is worthy of remark, that the wifeft men are feldom great laughers. It fhould feem, that their modefty will not allow them an extravagant joy; and I have

known

known wife men, who have preferred the
tears of Heraclitus to the laughter of
Democritus. It may not be amifs here
to inform the more youthful part of my
readers, that Heraclitus was a philofopher
who wept for the follies of mankind, and
that Democritus was alfo a philofopher,
who, on the contrary, laughed at every
thing he faw.

Hiftory produces many inftances, in
which the excefs of laughter has been
carried fo far as to occafion inftant death.
Valerius Maximus makes mention of one
Philemon, who having ordered a bafket
of figs to be brought to him, was highly
diverted on feeing an afs eat them all,
and immediately ordered that they fhould
pour down the animal's throat fome wine,
that the figs might not give him the cholic.
This ftrange caprice threw him into fuch
a fit of laughter as proved his immediate
death.

Cœlius Rodiginus fpeaks of a fimilar
fool, named Zeuxis, a famous painter,
who, having painted an old woman in a
fingular

fiingular posture, was so struck with the conceit, that death alone was capable of putting an end to his laughter. This is a kind of death as ridiculous as it is unusual; for few men laugh on taking leave of this world: the greater part take their farewel with tears in their eyes, and sorrow in their souls.

EDUCATION.

THE education of a child resembles the culture of plants. It is a soil, in which the infancy of man being sown, produces good or bad fruits, according to the good or bad qualities of the earth. The good grapes we with so much pleasure gather in the Autumn, cost us much care and pains in the spring. Thus, as the good or bad conduct of a man depends principally on his education, a father is obliged, according to the law of nature, to take all possible care, that his child, during his tender years, may imbibe sentiments of the love of virtue, and detestation of vice. This is very easily accomplished during

C 3

their

their infant ftate, which, like wax, receives every impreffion we wifh to give it.

Thus, as cuftom is fecond nature, fo virtue becomes natural to man, and cannot eafily be abandoned. It is the fame thing with vice, which, by the negligence or pernicious indulgence of parents, having once found a feat in the heart of a youth, is driven from thence with great labour and difficulty.

It fhonld feem, that the whole duty of a parent towards his child, is to give him a good education, and to put him, on his entrance on the commerce of the world, into the road that leads to fortune. Having done this, he has fulfilled all the duties of a parent; but to make himfelf unhappy in the purfuit of wealth, to deprive himfelf of the comforts of this life, and to make it a point of his duty to leave large poffeffions at his death, is a fpecies of madnefs and folly. The generality of children receive more pleafure and advantage in the poffeffion of what
they

they have acquired themfelves, than they do from that which is left them.

MAGNIFICENT DRESS.

IT has been obferved in all ages, that men of the greateft fenfe and abilities have defpifed magnificent dreffes, and that the pomp of comedians has feldom fuited their tafte. It is certain, that true virtue derives its luftre from itfelf, and refufes to receive any affiftance from gold or filver, which are invented only to pleafe children, fools, and coxcombs, who generally judge of mankind by the quantity of lace, with which their clothes are covered.

The man, who has real merit, generally choofes a plain drefs, fince it gives a luftre to virtue, and defpifes thofe embroidered and laced articles, which are much better calculated to cover the body of a horfe or a mule, than to ferve as a troublefome load to the human frame. Neatnefs becomes every one : it is generally the index of a man who is punctual

and

and exact in all his affairs, in the same manner as exceffive expences in coftly apparel are a mark of great want of fenfe, and evidently prove, that the wearer has no other means of attracting attention. Hence he obtains the admiration of the giddy and unthinking, and the contempt of the wife and prudent.

It has been obferved, that dwarfs, cripples, and thofe to whom nature has been deficient in fome part of her gifts, are generally the moft given to the parade of drefs. Their notions are certainly founded on the abfurdeft principles; for, in wifhing to diftinguifh themfelves by ornaments, they draw the attention of every one to the defects of their body, whereas, were they contented with a plain and decent drefs, thofe defects, from motives of humanity, might have been difregarded by the generality of the world. Some people have, indeed, made their fortune by the parade of drefs; and thefe have been generally thofe who have fought their fortune in the butterfly

circles

circles of kings and princes. Such men, however, owe more to chance and their taylor, than to prudence and good fenfe.

Laftly, it muft be allowed, that there are great marks of effeminacy in the excefs of drefs, and that a too complaifant attention to the prevailing fafhions is the effect of a ridiculous foftnefs. Cæfar, being warned by his friends to have a ftrict eye on Marc Antony and Dolabella, who were forming fome confpiracy againft him, replied, " I have little diftruft of thofe people who feed well and decorate their perfons; I have more fufpicion of thofe who are pale, meagre, and negligent of their drefs," meaning Brutus and Caffius, who were never frequenters of the fhops of lacemen, nor remarkably devoted to their taylors. The parade of drefs fhould be confined to actors on the theatres, and to thofe who have their fortune to feek only among women.

AMBITION.

AMBITION.

IT is natural for great fouls to wifh to procure immortality to their names, in order that a fomething may remain of them after their earthly diffolution, to collect laurels, and to make them the objects of admiration to posterity. Pliny the Younger made this confeffion: " I confefs, (faid he) that nothing employs my mind more than the extreme defire I have of immortalifing my name, fince fuch appears to me to be a defign worthy of a man of honour and virtue. He, who knows his life to be free from reproach, fears not to have it handed down to posterity."

Certain it is, that the defire of fhining in hiftory, of handing down our names to future ages, and to ftrive to acquire immortality by virtue, is a paffion worthy of great men. To obtain that happy end, we find pleafure in pain, we rejoice under fatigues, defpife dangers, and even brave death itfelf. It is certain, that
fuch

such a difposition muft be fomething more than human, and that the foul of an hero difplays the cleareft fentiments of contempt for every thing that does not tend to immortalife his name.

Virtue ferves as a fpur to the ambition of thefe great men, and hence it is not aftonifhing, that they wifh for no other recompence than a lafting remembrance of their glorious exploits. It is natural to abhor finking into eternal oblivion. He who dies without having done fomething noble and virtuous, which may preferve him in the memory of the living, is entirely forgotten as foon as his prefence is wanting to remind us of him. Men render their names immortal by illuftrious actions, ferve as models to great men in future ages, and, befides having their names refpected by pofterity, they have the pleafure to forefee, that their own defcendants will venerate their exiftence.

So powerful was the love of virtue in the remoteft ages of antiquity, of which hiftory furnifhes us with many examples,
that

that even in thofe days, when not an idea of the immortality of the foul exifted, men wifhed to immortalife their names by illuftrious actions. This cannot appear aftonifhing; but it is really furprifing, that any man fhould wifh to preferve his name to pofterity by an infamous action, like Heroftratus, who burned the temple of Diana at Ephefus, in order that his name might not be forgotten. However, there is a great difference between the memory of a virtuous hero, and that of an incendiary or affaffin. It is like viewing two different portraits; the one reprefenting Marcus Curtius, who was a voluntary victim to fave his country, and the other Nero, who killed his own mother out of wantonnefs:—the firft infpires our love and veneration, the other our horror and contempt.

REASON.

REASON is a proper rectitude of mind, which, when joined to wifdom,

ferves

ferves to regulate our conduct in the purfuits of this life. Wifdom confifts in the knowledge of divine and human things; it teaches us a due reverence to God, and inftructs us in what is ufeful for the general good of mankind.

Temperance, juftice, prudence, and generofity, are the effects of wifdom, but prudence claims the pre-eminence; fince, by her affiftance, reafon triumphs over the paffions. Pleafure and pain are equally blended with all the other paffions, for defire precedes pleafure, and joy ends it; fear precedes grief, and forrow comes as its companion.

Reafon being the compafs by which men ought to direct their courfe in the commerce of this world, the wife confult it in all their actions, and are thereby enabled to triumph over every thing that oppofes its power. Nature has given it to man as a prerogative which places him above all other animals, that it may ferve him as a guide to his conduct. Without reafon, he cannot find the true

D   road

road to felicity, which is enveloped in the dark and gloomy clouds every where spread by the follies and vices of this world. The fool, being ignorant of the value of reason, suffers the vanities and false pleasures of life to lead him astray, and thus becomes a prey to his own naturally bad dispositions.

The power of reason is very great when fortified by the knowledge of God, and by obedience to his laws. It was reason that supported the chastity of Joseph in the severe hour of trial, and corrected the boiling impetuosity of youth. Innumerable are the instances of this sort; but we shall conclude with observing, that there is no passion which reason cannot conquer, when it is left to itself to act freely.

CIVILITY.

CIVILITY is the consequence of a good education, and the true mark of a polite parentage. It has the property of attracting the good opinion of people

at

at a little expence, and even brutality
yields to its power. It cofts nothing,
and often procures us the greateft advantages. It is certain, that civility has
extraordinary effects; for it forces men
to be honeft, makes avarice afhamed of
itfelf, foftens the favage heart, and keeps
the clown at a distance. To a great
prince, it is as an invaluable diamond in
his crown; among the nobility, it is
a precious ornament; and among the
vulgar, it is a wonder if ever found.
It is a great recommendation to a literary
man, and often procures more honour
thereby than from his literary abilities.

However, as appearances are often
deceitful, the exceffive civility of a man
is fometimes fufpected by the wife; for
it is not uncommon to meet with that fort
of people, who load with civilities thofe
whom they mortally hate. Perhaps, the
fureft method is, to meafure the civilities
we receive from others by our own
merits, and to accept of no more of it
than is due to us, but to regard

the reft as raillery, or as a fnare laid
to entrap us.

FIRMNESS OF MIND.

IT is from the hand of Firmnefs, con-
ftancy, or ftability, call it by which name
you will, that virtue receives her crown
of glory. It ftands immoveable as a
rock, againft which the furious billows
of the ocean vent all their rage in vain,
and is proof againft all the viciffitudes of
this world. Indeed, there is fomething
divine in the virtuoufly-refolute mind;
for it is always the fame, and does not,
camelion like, attract the colours of
every thing that furrounds it.

Firmnefs reprefents a faint image of
eternity, and is the perfection of all the
virtues, fince without the affiftance of
the former, the latter could have no
ftability. Before Firmnefs, all the bad
influences lofe their force; for it teaches
us to fupport the ills of life without
regarding their weight. It is a fure
pledge of a happy futurity, and is happinefs

pinefs in itfelf. It regrets not the paft, nor ftands in fear of the future ; for it forefees events that are to happen. Fortune has no power over it, and the arrows of chance, whatever they may be, cannot pierce it. It fears nothing from the change of times, for it is always the fame till its final diffolution.

INSTABILITY.

MEANNESS under misfortunes, and infolence in profperity, are derived from the fame fource. An excefs of fenfibility in the mind, humbled by the unexpected reverfe of fortune, endeavours by meannefs to excite compaffion, being the only power it is capable of exerting, with any hopes of fuccefs. On the other hand, infolent profperity, fupported by felf-love fo natural to man, prefents to his imagination the idea of fuperiority derived from fortune, which makes him place himfelf in a rank fuperior to the reft of mankind.

D 3

The

' The firſt unqueſtionably is the mark of a degenerate ſoul, though the world in general conſider it as prudence; and the ſecond is a ridiculous folly, though they may chriſten the pride of the favourite of fortune by the name of a noble haughtineſs. No ſenſible perſon can approve either the one or the other; for to change from meanneſs to inſolence, or from inſolence to meanneſs, according to the different circumſtances of life, mark the ſlavery of a ſoul to the paſſions of a corrupt heart.

' The noble and generous ſoul deſpiſes being mean in adverſity, as much as it does inſolence in proſperity. It feels nothing from the humiliating ſhocks of misfortune, nor is puffed up by the inſolence of proſperity, but always remains tranquil and compoſed in every condition, being fully perſuaded, that man is but a ſhadow, and life but a dream.

ENVY.

ENVY.

OF the feven mortal fins, Envy is one, which troubles moft the repofe of mankind; and as it has its root in the excefs of felf-love, it is no wonder, that its venomous fruits poifon the repofe of the geneiality of mortals. Envy induced the arch enemy of mankind to feek the means of deftroying the felicity of our firft parents; and, probably, from the moment they eat of the forbidden fruit, this horrid vice paffed from the Devil into man, not only to deftroy thofe into whom it firft entered, but to be the rock, on which millions of men have fplit when they leaft expected it.

When we examine the envious man, he appears to refemble a denron, better than any other copy that can be traced of that original; and if we can in this world form any ideas of eternal punifh-ments, the envious man can, from his own feelings, give us fome account of them. So great is his diforder, that the

happinefs

happinefs of others encreafes it; and, if he be capable of receiving any comfort, it can be only from the misfortunes of his neighbours,

It feems to the envious man, that the happinefs of another is a robbery committed on him, and that fortune has been guilty of a crime in neglecting him. He is hungry when he knows that another man eats, and the cold freezes him in proportion as another is warmed. He is night and day reftlefs in inventing obftacles to oppofe the happinefs of others, and his foul knows no joy but in the deftruction and ruin of his neighbour. His two greateft favourites are lies and falfehoods, and he feeds on his own heart, which he gnaws night and day. His eyes appear like furies, and his hair is compofed of ferpents. His mouth is the entrance of the infernal regions, and his ears the receptacle of falfe echoes. His hands are the claws of a tyger, and his feet thofe of a horfe, which are perpetually kicking. His breath is a devouring

The Envious Man.

vouring flame, and his words are cutting
razors. Laftly, he is deferted by God,
execrable to men, and the darling of the
Devil.—My pen ftops fhort with horror.

THE SOVEREIGN GOOD.

THE ancient philofophers had different opinions concerning what confti-
tuted the happinefs of man, and what
they commonly called the fovereign good.
Efchines placed it in fleep; Pindar
maintained, that it confilted in health;
Zeno believed, that it was found in the
crown, which they placed on the head
of him, who carried the prize in the
combats; the Corinthians placed it in
gaming; Epicurus in voluptuoufnefs,
and many others placed it in honours,
riches, and dignities; but Ariftotle confidered it as confifting of virtue and
wifdom.

It is, however, clearly evident, that
among the Pagans, who had no knowledge of the immortality of the foul,
each naturally placed the fovereign good
in

in that which moft flattered his ruling paffion. Since the greater part of the things of this world have no value in themfelves, it is the imagination of each particular that muft fix their price.

Efchines, for example, was undoubtedly a phlegmatic and indolent man : he confequently believed that the fovereign good confifted in fleep, which his habit of body made him prefer to every thing elfe.

Pindar, who feems to have been of a weak and fickly conftitution, could not make ufe of great exertions, and therefore preferred health to all other things.

Zeno, undoubtedly the fon of a prizefighter, loved manual fports, and placed the fovereign good in the fuperior knowledge of boxing and wreftling.

The Corinthians, who were a lazy and worthlefs people, placed all their felicity in gaming ; witnefs Chilo, one of the feven wife men of Greece, who arriving one day at their city, found them

them all engaged in thofe ridiculous employments.

Epicurus, the true friend to good living and voluptuoufnefs, placed his happinefs in the gratification of the fenfes.

Ariftotle, who had fome ideas of the immortality of the foul, placed the fovereign good in virtue and wifdom. It is not at all furprizing, that this philofopher fhould have fentiments fo juft; for, having fome ideas of a fecond life, he could not think in the rude manner of his ignorant cotemporaries.

It is not a little furprifing, that among all the philofophers and men of great genius, which antiquity has produced, none of them have thought of placing the fovereign good in *indifference*, fince, when it is fincere, it places man in a ftate of equality, and raifes him above every agitation, which the revolutions of time can give to mortals. It fhould feem that a Pagan, who knows nothing of the immortality of the foul, and who
looks

looks for nothing beyond tranquillity, which is the moſt pleaſing of all the vanities of this world, would place the ſovereign good in indifference.

CONFIDENCE.

IT is certain, that we cannot be too circumſpect in our choice of the perſon we mean to make our confident, and entruſt with the ſecrets of our hearts; for, generally ſpeaking, we make our-ſelves the ſlaves of thoſe, to whom we open the ſecrets of our boſoms. A good and generous heart too often and too eaſily opens itſelf, which is frequently taken advantage of by the artful, treache-rous, and falſe friend.

The temper of mankind is ſo incon-ſiſtent, that he, who to-day loads us with careſſes, may to-morrow conceive for us a hatred, which breathes nothing but our ruin: ſo that the confidence we have placed in a perſon, whom we con-ſidered as a valuable friend, may one day, when his ſentiments for us change,

I   forge

forge those words, which we have incautiously entrusted him with, into arrows that may deeply wound us. The daily experience this world affords us, admits no doubt of the truth of this observation. However great our friendship or esteem may be of any man, prudence directs us to be very cautious, and to make our own bosoms only the repository of the latent secrets of our hearts. The old proverb truly says, " The words of a wife man lie at the root of his tongue; but those of a fool play on the tip of it."

BRAVERY.

BRAVERY and Liberality are two qualities which seldom fail to attract the esteem of mortals: the first displays a contempt of life, and the second regards riches with an eye of indifference: two things, to which men in common shew the strongest attachment.

However, the excess of either merits contempt; for, whenever we lose sight of prudence, the first becomes temerity,

E   and

and the second prodigality : two vices as prejudicial to our happiness as, they are contemptible in the eyes of the wise. Temerity prevents a man from thinking of the true value of life, and exposes him to the dangers of death on the most trifling occasions; while prodigality, not reflecting on the bitterness of want, prostitutes itself to contempt, inseparable from poverty. When bravery is not accompanied by the virtues, it places a man in an aukward situation, since courage can be displayed only against enemies. When the sword of war is sheathed, bravery then languishes.

History is full of the heroic and illustrious actions of great men. Those of the famous Prince de Condé, under the reign of Lewis the Fourteenth, merit esteem; but much more do I admire the bravery of Viscount Turenne, who shone as much by his prudence, as the other dazzled the eyes of the public by his rash exploits. Condé was said to have an eye on the throne; but too

much

much fire reduced his projects to smoke.
Turenne supported his character by va-
lour, prudence and generosity. Condé,
after having braved death in a thousand
shapes, at last died peaceably in his bed in
an advanced age ; whereas Turenne, without ever having rashly exposed his person
to danger, was killed by a cannon ball.
The decrees of God are impenetrable.—
Let us always adore them.

A GOOD HEART.

THERE is no qualification of a human
being more to be prized than that of a
good heart ; for besides being a source of
true felicity to him who possesses it, it is a
treasure to those who come within the
reach of its beneficent and generous influence.

A good heart feels for the misfortunes
of others, and commiserates all those
whom inability prevents him from assisting. He, who possesses a good heart,
puts the best face upon little errors, and
is ingenious in concealing the defects of

E 2 mankind.

mankind. He confiders the misfortunes of his neighbour as a letter of recommendation, and endeavours to perfuade himfelf, that mifery is a facred thing. If his eyes be fhut to the weaknefſes of others, his ears are alſo deaf to the malevolent infinuations of evil minds. His tongue moves only in the praiſes of every one, and he is mute when called upon to fupport the maledictions of others. He endeavours to promote univerſal felicity, and fincerely rejoices when he has it in his power to extend it. It is with regret he fees differences among friends, and he fpares neither time nor pains to bring them to a right underſtanding with each other. He endeavours to foften the rage of the paſſionate man, and is ftruck with horror at the idea of every act of revenge. He knows not what envy is, and wifhes well to all the world. He comforts the afflicted, and does not, in any fhape, add to the load of misfortunes. Indeed, a good heart may be called the perfection of of the virtues, and the prefage of a happy eternity.

It is to be lamented, that, in our age, the goodnefs of the heart is little in fafhion; but this arifes from the general corruption of manners, and that vice now impudently affumes the name of virtue, and that moft virtues pafs for a fignal of weaknefs.

INTEREST.

INTEREST is the principal end of the greater part of the actions of mankind, and all ranks of people are fubject to its influence. It is the purfuit of every one, and is the only machine that puts things in motion. To fuch a height is its influence raifed in thefe days, that among moft mortals it is fuffered to take place of fenfe and reafon, fince every action, which has not intereft for its object, is confidered as indifcreet and abfurd. Self - intereft, however, when it lofes fight of truth, reafon, and juftice, is a moft pernicious quality,

E 3   dangerous

dangerous to the community at large, and proclaims its poſſeſſor to be a vicious perſon.

" Intereſt (ſays an ingenious French writer) appears to me to reſemble duſt, which the demon throws into the eyes of men, in order to make them blind to juſtice, duty, honour, and friendſhip. It is Intereſt that ſtifles the natural ſentiments of relations for each other, embroils man and wife, ſows the ſeeds of hatred among brothers and ſiſters, and extinguiſhes friendſhip among friends. The great make uſe of it as a pretence to commit the moſt unjuſt actions, and to the vulgar it ſerves as an excuſe for diſſolving the tie of obedience they owe to their ſovereign. It makes courtiers ſlaviſh, ſoldiers raſh, eccleſiaſtics hypocritical, and merchants deceitful. Thus it becomes the maſter of the other paſſions, often ſubdues them, and leads them in triumph. In public, it aſſumes the name of prudence, but privately it ſtoops to any meanneſs or injuſtice that can promote its ends."

FORTUNE

FORTUNE CHANGES THE MAN.

" HONOURS change our manners,
(fays a noble Roman writer) but not
always for the better." It is fo common
a thing in the commerce of this world to
fee men, who rife to honours and riches,
change their behaviour, temper, views,
and inclinations, that we are not at all
furprifed at it.

What a folly to forget ourfelves, to be
no more found, merely from having
changed fituation! What injuftice to
neglect old friends on the empty parade
of a new fortune! It is in fact telling all
the world, that he is not deferving of his
fortune ; and that the imaginary felicity
of riches is preferable to the real enjoyments of virtue.

We may fay, that the acquifition of a
fortune is of no fervice to the memory,
fince we frequently obferve, that the
happy man forgets to-day the perfon who
yefterday affifted him, and knows not
even the name of him, who helped him
in

in the beginning of his career of fortune. As gold is proved by the fire, so is man by prosperity, If the former properly stands the assay, and the latter preserves its integrity amidst honours, they may be then said to have arrived at a state of perfection.

Great God! how miserable is the lot of man! In prosperity, he forgets every one; and in adversity, every one forgets him. In prosperity he appears to have lost his senses; and when loaded with misfortunes, he is said never to have had any, In his sudden elevation, he becomes discontented with all the world; and, when hurled to the bottom of the wheel of fortune, all the world are discontented with him. He who basks in the sun-shine of fortune should remember, that riches sometimes take the wing, and suddenly fly away from us. Happy is he who reflects, that old money, old wine, old books, and old friends, are objects worthy the attention of every man of good sense.

LIBERALITY.

LIBERALITY.

EVERY one who is in the poffeffion of wealth, has it in their power to do much good; but it does not always happen, that thofe who have it in their power, know how properly to ufe it. It is a fecret referved for noble fouls, who confider the perfon, the time, and manner, of properly conferring a favour. Whereas there are many people who give difguft by the manner in which they do a kindnefs, and lofe the merit of it by the aukward mode of doing it. People who affect to be generous, never give but with oftentation; but true liberality is always the fame, whetl er it be in private, or in the face of the whole world.

There are others, who, confidering themfelves as under the neceffity of affuming the character of liberality, act in fo proud and haughty a manner, that the favours they beftow rather encreafe the affliction than relieve the neceffities of thofe who receive them. True liberality
is

is always performed in such a maner as to
enhance the value of the gift.   It is only
true and genuine generosity, that knows
how properly so to season its gifts, as to
render them palatable and pleasing to all
who partake of them.

HOPE.

WE cannot but consider Hope as a
strong mark of the Divine pity; for, after
the fatal fall of our first parents, which
entailed upon us all the miseries of this
painful life, how could we be able to
support them without the hope of a
change? In true hope, which is the
consolation of the unfortunate, is the only
support of mortals in this world; for
that revives the most dejected spirits, and
whatever evils may befall a man, so long
as hope accompanies him, it will not fail
to support him.   Like some powerful
cordials, of which but a few drops serve
to strengthen the heart, however weak it
may be, it has the virtue of encouraging
those who, amidst the adversities of this
life,

life, are in want of courage to persevere to the end of their mortal career. Poverty, sickness, persecution, and all the other ills of this life, are softened by hope.

FLATTERY.

A PHILOSOPHER being one day asked, which were the most formidable animals to men, he replied, "Among savages, it is the slanderer; and in domestic life, the flatterer." Certain it is, that the flatterer unites in his character many infamous vices; for he is a liar, in speaking those things which he does not believe; he is deceitful, in speaking contrary to his sentiments; he is a coward, not daring to speak what he thinks; he is wicked, because he pours oil on the fire of the self-love of another; he is impious, in praising the vices of his neighbour; and he is the enemy of those he calls his friends, since by his flattery he encourages them in their evil courses.

Flattery is a sweet venom, with which the great are poisoned, who are too often persuaded,

perfuaded, that their vices are only imper-
fect virtues. It is aftonifhing, that to fuch
a height has this vice got in courts, that,
without flattery, no man can there hope
for any fuccefs. Indeed, felf-love muft
have obtained a powerful dominion over
the heart of man, fince it fuffers us to receive the incenfe we do not merit, and
makes us like the flatterer, who mocks our
underftanding, by attributing to us thofe
qualities we do not poffefs. Nothing is
more univerfal than to hear men exclaim
againft flatterers; but there are very few
people who quarrel with a man for telling
him too much of his own merits and underftanding. In fhort, there are fome
paffions that will leave us as we advance in
age, but the love of flattery will purfue us
to the grave.

FAMILIARITY.

TO know how to keep familiarity at
a proper diftance from the commerce of
friendfhip, is a fcience, to which the world
do not pay the attention it merits. To
fhew

shew its ineftimable value we need only remark, that it is to this science that friendfhip is indebted for its duration. Friendfhip is founded on efteem, and efteem is a tribute due to merit, but as every man has his weakneffes, familiarity foon difcovers them, and imprudently checks them, without confidering, that the felf-love of every man is wounded when we bear hard on his foibles; and thus the good harmony between friends is frequently interrupted.

Sympathy forms friendfhip, complaifance nourifhes it, and integrity of heart preferves it; but excefs of familiarity often does fo much injury to friendfhip, as even to diffolve it. Every man, who fays, that familiarity is the enfign of friendfhip, is not acquainted with the delicacy of the latter; and he, who is too fond of our familiarity, feldom cares much about our friendfhip. Familiarity opens the door to love, but fhuts it againft friendfhip. He who wifhes to make friendfhip lafting, fhould fo manage that

F delicate

delicate bufinefs, that exceffive familiarity
fhould not be fuffered to appear; for that
mother never fails to introduce her daughter contempt, who is the fource of irre-
concileable enmity..

INEQUALITY OF TEMPER.

A FRIEND of an irregular Temper
is like good provifions badly cooked;
for his happy moments, being frequently
interrupted by caprice, prevent us from
tranquilly enjoying the pleafures of his
friendfhip.

A man of an unfettled temper never
follows even his own will, and confequently we never can difcover what are
his refolutions, he every moment changing
his opinion. He is incapable of great
affairs, and difagreeable even in fmall
concerns. It is with difficulty he finds
friends, and it is impoffible for him to
keep them. An irregular temper is the
mark of a weak judgment, fince it fhews
to-day, by marks of indifference, the
regret it feels of being yefterday deceived

in

In its choice, and that coolnefs, which fo
clofely follows careffes, is infinitely more
mortifying to a generous mind, than the
firft demonftrations of his friendſhip gave
it pleafure.

An irregular-tempered man is like a
baftard plant, whom nature has not taken
the pains to perfeɑ. When we happen
to be conneɑed with a man of this
charaɑer, the beft way perhaps would be
to confider him in the light of a comedian,
who at one time reprefents a king, and at
another time a beggar; fometimes a
philofopher, and fometimes a harlequin;
fometimes a lamb, and fometimes a bear.
It is only mere pafs-time we can hope to
receive from a man of an unfettled temper,
fince no dependance can be placed on him
as a friend.

RARITIES.

EVERY thing this world produces is
imperfeɑ, the poffeffion of them diminifhes their value, and even the hope of
acquiring we know not what is often at-
F 2

tended

tended with infinitely greater anxiety, than the poſſeſſion of what we have ſo ardently purſued gives us pleaſure. The value we put upon things merely on ac-count of their difficulty to be obtained is abſurd; ·for we ſhould certainly fix the price on them only in proportion to their utility. It is evidently a proof of our weakneſs, to give the preference to any thing merely becauſe it is the growth of a foreign country. Reaſon naturally dic-tates to us, that any thing really uſeful to us, and the product of our own country, muſt be more valuable in itſelf, with re-ſpect to us, than any uſeleſs commodity imported from the Indies.

Pearls are of little value in the Eaſt, gold at Peru, or odoriferous drugs in Arabia; but here they are eſteemed at a high price, merely on account of their ſcarcity with us. However, it is our own imagination only that enhances their price; and, to ſpeak the truth, the Eu-ropeans are more fooliſh ſo much to eſteem gold, which is only a yellow earth,
and

and pearls, which are but a kind of fhell-fifh, than were the Indians, who fo dearly paid the Dutch for the firft cat they carried among them, fince that animal was of more fervice to them in killing their mice, than all the gold and pearls of the Eaft.

It is true, that gold at this day will do many things, not to fay every thing, with refpeft to vanity and avarice ; but, as gold could not drive away mice, fo in that country a cat was certainly of more value than gold.

For my own part, I muft confefs, that I prefer the magpie in his half-mourning drefs, when he has learned to imitate the human voice, to the proud peacock, with all the brilliant plumage of his tail, fince he utters only difcordant and difagreeable founds.

Nature has been fo juft in the divifion of her gifts, that fhe has beftowed on each country whatever is neceffary to fupply its wants, provided they know how to be contented with the real neceffaries of

F 3   life,

life, without being obliged to vifit foreign countries. As all kinds of fuperfluities are ufclefs, fo things however fcarce, which ferve only to feed our vanity and encreafe our luxury, appear to me of no value, even though they may be brought from the remoteft regions of the earth.

A plain family joint of Englifh beef is certainly preferable to a turtle, which is made to pleafe the palate by the addition of wines and foreign fpices, without the affiftance of which it would be rejected with contempt. After all, every one has his predominant tafte.

NAVIGATION.

OF all the elements, water is perhaps the leaft to be trufted, fince a calm is often a forerunner of a furious tempeft, and juftly verifies the old proverb, that *danger lurks on the brink of fecurity.* Cato ufed to fay, he repented of three things: of having fuffered a day to pafs without doing fome good; of having entrufted a fecret to an improper perfon; and

and of venturing on the water when he might have gone by land.

- Another Roman ufed to fay, that a fhip was the emblem of madnefs, becaufe it was never a moment in one fituation; that the mariner was a fool, becaufe he changed his opinion with every wind; that the water was a fool, becaufe it never was at reft; and that the wind was a fool, becaufe it was never fteady to one point; to which we may add, that it is the height of folly to join in fuch company.

There is, indeed, no profeffion more perilous than that of a feaman, fince his life is every moment feparated from death only by a fingle plank. He has often the four elements to ftruggle with at one time, and fometimes is burnt alive in the midft of water. His principal end is to arrive at land, and yet the fight of that element, in fome fituations, drives him to defpair. Though he refts all his hopes on the winds, yet thofe very winds frequently prove his deftruction. Laftly, he

feeks

feeks riches, and inftead of them fometimes meets with unhappinefs, mifery, and
even death itfelf.

Notwithftanding all this, navigation is
one of the fineft and moft ufeful fciences
that man ever difcovered; for, befides
the riches it introduces into every country, it ferves to draw the wonders of the
Creator from the mafs of ignorance, by
the knowledge it has given us of fo
many different regions, nations, religions,
manners, animals, fruits, and plants. So
that, every thing confidered, we have
reafon to thank Heaven for having given
birth to men of fo rude a tafte, as con-
tentedly to live on ftockfifh and bifcuits,
in order to furnifh others, from the four
quarters of the world, with the delicacies
of the remoteft regions, and every moment to run the rifk of their lives, to
procure to the luxurious the delicacies of
the table.

GAMING.

GAMING.

IT is faid that the Lydians were the firft inventors of gaming, in order to amufe themfelves when they could get no provifions to eat. If that be true, their lofs of time was not badly employed; but as daily experience proves to us the contrary, and that we every day fee people whom the madnefs of gaming expofes to famine and death, we cannot but treat with contempt the memory of thofe fluggards who firft invented it. Indeed, when we reflect on the various misfortunes that gaming draws on itfelf, it appears to me, that it would be very difficult to afcertain its firft inventor; unlefs it be the demon himfelf, who, by the means of gaming, encreafed his empire of the robbers of time and of the purfe.

I perfectly agree with thofe who will infift, that an innocent game may fometimes amufe and relieve the mind, for a little time, from the moft painful purfuits

suits in the commerce of this world: it is against the use of it in excess that reason and conscience revolt. Mahomet very properly forbid his disciples all games of chance; nor was that Turk wrong, who laughed at two Christians who were *amusing* themselves by playing for money; " What a folly! (said he) for two men to take money out of their pockets, and put it to hazard to which it belongs!" At any rate, the character of a gamester is at all times despicable, since they are principally composed of thieves and sharpers.

CRUELTY.

A SOUL truly generous can never be cruel, since cruelty harbours only in the bosom of a mean tyrant. Ferocity is repugnant to human nature, and converts him in whom it is found to a monster, and a declared enemy of society. A cruel prince is the plague of nations, and sent by God as a scourge upon mankind; and, perhaps, comes to the

same

fame end as do those rods which the tender parent throws into the fire, after he has used them to correct his child.

All the world wishes ill to a tyrant, and even those who are not under his yoke pray for his ruin : God abhors him, and his own conscience will be one day his executioner. As his joy consisted in the affliction of others, his ruin will rejoice his people, when divine justice shall deliver them from the gripe of that Nero.

History is replete with accounts of the unfortunate end of tyrants, whom a violent and premature death has hastened to the grim regions of Pluto, where they will be treated with an indulgence similar to that they have granted to others, and where the sighs of those, whom they afflicted and tormented in this life, will fan the fire of their torments. Lastly, every cruel person, be his condition either exalted or humble, must expect punishment either in this or the other world,

and

and often in both, since the same measure we make to others will be again measured to us.

AVARICE.

THERE is hardly a vice more oppo-site to good sense than this; for the ava-ricious man prostitutes his honour, his life, and even his soul, merely to hoard up treasures, from which he derives no other advantage than the pain of taking care of it, the uneasy fears of losing it, and the injustice he makes use of to encrease it. The miser thinks himself master of his riches, but does not perceive that he is the slave to them. He bears them so high a respect, that he presumes only to touch them; he loves nobody, and no-body loves him, nor does he even love himself. In proportion as he fills his chests, his poverty encreases; so that, like a second Tantalus, while in the arms of opulence he experiences all the horrors of poverty.

It

The Avaricious Man.

It is without doubt the evident effects of the divine juſtice againſt this vice, that the avaricious man condemns himſelf not to make uſe of his riches, and is a prey to the devouring idea, that he muſt leave all his riches to his heirs, whoſe moſt ardent wiſh is to ſee him in his grave.

I remember to have read, that a certain biſhop was ſo avaricious that he went by night to rob his own horſes of their oats; and that this prelate, of ſo exemplary a life, was one night ſeized by his groom, who, under cover of the dark, worked hard with a good cudgel on the ſhoulders of his maſter, ſuppoſing him to be ſome needy thief.

Avarice is a vice, from which even the demon himſelf is exempt, though its pro-feſſors contribute greatly to enlarge his empire. It muſt give great pleaſure to the evil ſpirit, to ſee how man abandons his God for ſo vile a thing as gold, and difregard his falvation to become a ſlave to that yellow earth, which he muſt leave behind him.

G　　　　　　　　*DEATH.*

DEATH.

DEATH having been introduced into the world by Sin, it is not all surprising, that there should be something frightful in its appearance, even the very idea of which makes men tremble. Its effect is an incontestable proof of the punishment of crimes.

Terrible as it may be, it frees us from all the miseries of this life, and opens to us the gates of eternity. The death of a good man is the completion of his felicity; but that of a wicked man is the commencement of his misery.

When we properly consider the matter, we find a striking proof of the divine bounty even in our dissolution. It is the end of all the evils that accompany this life, which, were they for ever to endure, would be far more insupportable than even death itself. When we reflect on the miseries of old age, and that, after having seen sixty revolving suns, we generally begin to be a load to others as well as to ourselves;

ourfelves; what would that mifery be, were we doomed to live eternally loaded with all thofe calamities, which our firft parents drew on their unhappy pofterity by their difobedience? Certainly it would be an infupportable punifhment.

Since death is no more than a tribute we owe to nature, let us pay it without complaining, but always endeavour to be upon our guard. Let us ftudy to have a confcience pure and clear from reproach, in order that we may not be furprifed by death, and we fhall then know by a happy experience, that there is nothing fo terrible in death as is reprefented to us. It is by death that Martyrs have received the crown of glory, in changing this fhort life, full of adverfity and pain, for an eternity of incomprehenfible felicities.

EPITAPHS.

THE laft vanities of men are their epitaphs, and are often a furer proof of the pride of the living, than of the virtues of the dead. It fhould feem from hence,

that

that falfity is fo infeparably united to man, that it accompanies him even to his tomb, and triumphs over his afhes. The expence attending monumental erections is often only with a view to give credit to impofition; and the eulogiums which are engraved on marble in Honour of the deceafed, are too often only a portrait of what we would wifh they had refembled, rather than a faithful picture of what they had been.

Epitaphs are a gafconade of words, to which a judicious reader feldom gives any credit. If the foul, after it has taken its flight, be happy, it wants no pompous epitaphs here; and, if it be not happy, no expences whatever on a monument will mend its condition. Heirs, however, who through gratitude or friendfhip, employ certain fums in ornamenting the tombs of their relations and friends, appear more excufeable than thofe, who, during their lives, expend vaft fums in raifing magnificent maufoleums as repofitories of their dead carcafes, and who have the effrontery

to

to compofe an eulogium on their lives,
and thus make themfelves liars long after
they can no more fpeak.

THE DISTRIBUTIONS OF NATURE.

NATURE is fo juft in the diftriba-
tion of her favours to men, that fhe, in
fome meafure, rewards all her votaries.
If fhe gives to one man riches and
power, fhe adds to it a reftlefs and un-
bounded ambition; if another be poor
and unfortunate, fhe gives him patience
and contentment. If the firft with his
riches had the indifference of the latter,
he would certainly be too happy; and if
the latter had the natural inquietude of
the former added to his bad fortune, he
would affuredly have juft room to complain.

If we weigh then the riches of the firft
with the misfortunes of the fecond, and
the inquietude of the one with the contentment of the other, we fhall certainly
find the balance even; for the indifference

of

of the fecond laughs at the inquietude of the firft, and his patience is fo great, that his difgraces have no effect on him. Should time or accident happen to change the fortune of both of them, what a load of misfortunes would not the firft experience, if indigence fhould be affociated with his natural inquietude? The only prudent ftep we can take, is to make ourfelves eafy and quiet in whatever fituation Providence may have placed us.

HONOUR.

HONOUR refembles the eye, which cannot admit of the leaft impurity without receiving a material alteration. It is a precious ftone, the leaft defect in which diminifhes the price. It is a treafure, which, when once unfortunately loft, can never be recovered. As falvation is to the next life, fo is honour to this; the firft cannot be acquired but with great care, and the laft cannot be preferved but with the moft cautious delicacy. The
wife

wife confider it as a refource in every misfortune that may happen to them; whereas the fool pledges it every moment upon the moft trifling purpofes. As a body without a foul is a corpfe, fo is a man without honour, whom all the world fhuns with averfion as impure.

Honour is fo entirely united with itfelf, that it cannot fuffer a diminution in any of its parts, without hazarding its whole exiftence. From hence it arifes, that we never fee what may be called a half-honeft man; for, generally fpeaking, he who is fo unfortunate as to receive a check on his honour, foon becomes a complete bankrupt. Honour and life put to the balance will prove equally ponde-rous; but as foon as we take honour out of the fcale, life weighs no more than a feather.

PATIENCE.

THE fool confiders patience as the mark of a weak heart, and generally reprefents

reprefents it as the refource of a coward; but the wife confider it as a mark of true grandeur of foul. It fupports itfelf by hope, and is a ftranger to defpair, which is the portion of mean fouls. Patience is fo great a refource againft all kinds of misfortunes, that every evil lofes three parts of its effects by the proper ufe we make of patience; it combats them wherever it meets them, and generally triumphs at laft. It honourably refifts the greateft calamities in life, and foftens the feverity of our adverfities in fuch a manner as hardly to fuffer us to feel them. It is a virtue, which always carries its reward along with it; for thofe who practife it, never fail to feel its happy effects.

The Emperor Marcus Aurelius, fo re-markable for his temper and patience, often faid, that Cæfar obtained the Empire by the fword, Auguftus by defcent, Caligula by his father's merits, Nero by tyranny, Titus by the conqueft of Judea; but as for himfelf, though of a low ex-traction,

traction, he had obtained it by patience. Such is the superior influence of this virtue.

However weighty may be our burthens, they cannot crush us totally, so long as patience lends us its support, and conducts us by its friendly hand. As every thing in nature has its contrariety, so patience is opposite to despair. The Christians consider it as a gift from heaven, and the ancient philosophers regarded it as the last effort of a firm and generous soul.

Patience is nearly allied to courage, which cannot shew itself to advantage without enemies; in the same manner, this virtue disappears the moment adversities abandon us. Patience is a generous friend, for it never comes near us during prosperity; but the moment we are likely to sink under misfortunes, it never fails to present itself to us, and to offer us its assistance. Lastly, it supports us to the end of our career, crowns all our labours, and conducts us into those paths, which lead to a happy eternity.

READ.

READING.

ALL the employments of mankind in this world are only amusements, except those to which we are indebted for our daily bread : all the rest are but pass-times. Of all the amusements, there is certainly no one more agreeable or instructive than that of reading.

Plautus, the Poet and Philosopher, in the early part of his life, was much given to the vanities of the world, and, owing to the great vivacity which nature had given him, was very irregular in his conduct. He began his career of life in the capacity of a soldier, after which he tempted fortune on the hazardous ocean. He next learned the trade of a baker, then became a taylor, next a merchant, and continued his pursuits in a variety of other professions till he at last commenced a philosopher. Being one day asked, in which of his professions he had found the most satisfaction, he thus replied :—
" There is no condition, of which we
do

do not wish for a change; no post of
honour without danger, no riches without
labour and inquietude, no prosperity so
permanent as not to have an end, nor
any pleasure so agreeable as not at last
to tire us: so that, if I have ever
experienced any peace and tranquillity,
it is only since I have given myself to reading."

This philosopher was indeed very right
in making those just observations; for,
whatever other vanities of this world we
may be engaged in, we only encrease our
inquietude, our wants, our desires, and
solicitations. After having obtained and
experienced them all, a few moments of
enjoyment are sufficient to disgust us with
them. The principal reason of all this is,
that we never properly esteem that which
we possess, but sigh too much after the
enjoyments of others.

An application to reading delivers us
from all those agitations; for it learns us
to know the vanity of all things, since the
dead,

dead, who tells no falfities, teach and perfuade us by their experience. The folidity of their converfation is infinitely preferable to the flighty vivacity of the living. If we wifh to know what is neceffary for our good, they will inftruct us without hypocrify; if we have an inclination to learn the fciences, they will teach us them without fee; if we wifh to learn the maxims of ftates, they will explain them without oftentation; if prudence urges us to learn the principles of economy, they will voluntarily teach us; and if we are defirous to acquire theological knowledge, we may find it in thofe mafters without pride or parade.

Thefe are the advantages we owe to reading, by the means of which we are introduced to the familiarity of the moft illuftrious fages of antiquity. Befides thefe, we derive other advantages from reading; and thefe confift in turning our attention from the frequent and dangerous commerce with the living, and infenfibly accuftoming ourfelves to commune with
the

The two Roads through Life.

the dead. From hence we fhall learn, that though we may acquire immortality in the facred page of hiftory, our bodies after death will moulder into afhes, and that all our knowledge, power, and grandeur, will terminate with our mortal lives.

The Two Roads Men pursue in this Life.

THERE are only two roads to travel in this world, the one agreeable, and the other ufeful. The firft is trodden by thofe men who feek nothing but pleafure, and give themfelves up wholly to the falfe allurements of life. The fecond is frequented by the wife, who tread only on firm paths in their journey through life.

The paths of pleafure are agreeable to the view, being bordered on all fides by trees of fingular beauty, yielding fruits enchanting to the fight; but when we wifh to tafte them, we find they are like the apples of Sodom, and full of nothing but cinders. On advancing

H further,

further, we obferve fountains, which, inftead of water, pour out the moft exqui-
fite wines. On each fide of the path we
behold beautiful meadows, covered with
the choiceft flowers, though their fmell
is intoxicating. We fee charming fields
bordered by little hills, on which we
difcover magnificent palaces, with fra-
grant groves of oranges and other choice
fruits.

In thefe palaces they do nothing but
laugh and fing. In fome of them we fee
tables covered with the moft delicious
food; in others, beautiful women, who
receive every paffenger with open arms.
Here concerts are formed of the moft en-
rapturing mufic; there they join in the
lively dance, attended by operas, plays,
and various other entertainments. In fome
places we fee magnificent equipages; in
others, a kind of fair, where we fee a
thoufand trifles brilliantly ornamented, but
totally ufelefs.

The traveller, his mind being fafci-
nated by the fight of thefe trifles, keeps
ftill

ftill advancing, without recollecting, that
perhaps three parts of his life have paffed
fince he entered this path, when, all on a
fudden, he begins to feel himfelf fatigued
with the length of his journey : he then
finds himfelf obliged to crofs a frightful
defert to gain a little ftraw hut, at the entrance of which he perceives an old man
of a hideous afpect, meagre, and worn
down to a fkeleton ; whofe eyes are funk
into his head, his black hair, terminated
with grey, hang in wild confufion over his
fhoulders, and forms, on the whole, a moft
frightful fpectre.

He afks the name of that place, and
wifhes to know who the old man is. To
which the furly old keeper replies,—
" This is the country of Tears and Repentance, and my name is Mifery.—
I am placed here by the decrees of Heaven, to receive and lodge thofe travellers
who come here over the paths of Pleafure."

The poor ftranger, terrified at this an-
fwer, afks if there be no other place in
H 2   that

that neighbourhood where he can repofe himfelf? "Ah! (replies Mifery), at ten paces from hence lives my neighbour De-fpair; but I fincerely tell you, that of all thofe who have rather chofen to go to him, than to abide with me, not one has ever returned. It is, therefore, either with him or me, that you muft finifh the career of pleafures, in which you have been engaged."

As to the path of Utility, its entrance is more difficult. We begin it by climbing craggy mountains, in which we muft employ all the labour of our youth, be-fore we can hope to arrive at its moft lofty fummit. We muft fubmit to encounter every danger, by afcending the preci-pices we meet with on the way, without meeting with any other companions. than Labour and. Pain, who encourage his purfuits by the advantages and charms of Utility, receiving, at the fame time, fome affiftance from Hope, who perfuades him, that the remainder of his journey will be fhort. His own defires keep

pace

pace with the fincerity of Hope, and thus
fortified by the charms of thofe flattering
promifes, he regularly advances to the
height of this frightful mountain, on
which he fees, though at fome diftance, a
palace of enchanting ftructure, and moft en-
rapturing fituation.

He firft enquires after the name and
mafter of this beautiful edifice, when he
is told, that the firft is called Convenience,
and the fecond, Repofe. He haftens his
pace, and rejoices infinitely at this informa-
tion, hoping there to refrefh and repofe
himfelf after all his toils and fatigues.—
The mafter of the palace then affigns him
an apartment agreeable to his wifhes, and
Hope tells him, " Here end all your
fatigues and labours ; here you may
repofe in quiet for the remainder of your
days."

The poor traveller perceives an extraordinary joy glowing in his bofom, and
foon begins to form projects in his mind
of making himfelf mafter of the whole
palace. He fets his head to work, begins

to

'to be uneasy, and cannot be contented with the sweet apartment he possesses in this pleasing abode. Amidst these agitations of his mind, Death suddenly appears, who, with a terrible visage, makes a sign to him with his finger to follow him.— He endeavours to oppose his commands, complaining bitterly of the cruelty of being so soon obliged to quit his repose, which had cost him so much labour and pain to acquire; but Death, always inexorable, seizes him without pity, and hurls him into a pit of six feet deep, where, covered with earth, he becomes the prey of worms, and has no further recompence for his past labours, than a few words engraved on marble, which inform posterity, that such a man had lived according to the rules of prudence.—Vanity of vanities; all things are vanity!

I cannot, however, quit this subject without observing, that though the most prudent conduct, as well as the most flighty and futile, must at last come to an end, yet my youthful readers cannot but

observe,

obferve, from what has been here allego-
rically mentioned, that the path of Pleafure leads to Mifery and Defpair, and that
the path of Utility is terminated by the enjoyment of Convenience and Repofe. If
we do not make a proper ufe of the latter,
the fault refts only with ourfelves.

PRESUMPTION.

THE high opinion a man has of him-
felf is generally the effect of his little difcernment, which has not fufficient extent
to comprehend the merit of another; his
vanity being employed only in contem-
plating himfelf, he has not leifure to obferve what is brilliant in others. His
felf-love, which ferves him as a mirror,
every moment prefents to him fuch unri-
valled accomplifhments in himfelf, that his
imagination can find nothing in the reft of
mankind, that can enter into comparifon
with his wonderful talents.

When Alexander the Great was on
his death-bed, his courtiers befought him
to name his fucceffor; but that proud
                              monarch,

monarch, evidently confidering no perfon
as worthy to fucceed him, nominated neither his brother Arideus, nor his fons,
nor the infant, of which his wife Roxana
was then with child, but anfwered, that
he left the empire to him who fhould be
moft worthy of it; well knowing, that the
words, *the moft worthy*, would prove an
apple of contention among the great, and
that felf-vanity would not fail to perfuade
each of his captains, that he himfelf was
fuperior to the reft.—Alexander was
not deceived in his conjecture; for, after
his death, that vaft empire was torn in
pieces, divided among the great, and
was never afterwards reunited under
one chief, as Alexander had wifhed
it.

We may conclude with faying, that
Prefumption is the daughter of Pride,
and her mother the object of univerfal
hatred, even though fhe were accompanied with fome merit. As vanity
produces a contempt for others, fo the
vain

vain man cannot obtain the efteem of others. The vanity of a fool conftitutes a juft claim to a madhoufe.

The falfe Glare of a Crown.

NOTHING more perfectly fhews the equality of mankind than Death : it makes a prey of the rich as well as poor, and the monarch and the private man are frequently carried off by the fame kind of diforder. This fufficiently proves, that the greateft monarchs are compofed of no better materials than the meaneft of their fubjects, and that their crown, with all its brilliancy, and their fceptre with all its power, will have no influence with the grim king of terrors, Death.

No fooner has the foul quitted its prifon, than we conceive a horror and averfion to the body, to which, but a few moments before, we offered fo much incenfe, and to which we paid a refpect, approaching almoft to adoration. Monarchs are born to labour and pain as well

well as the reft of men. If we clofely examine the falfe brilliancy of their felicity, we fhall eafily perceive, that it is not proportioned to the cares and fatigues infeparable from a fceptre, without fpeaking of the continual rifques and dangers, to which they are expofed, as well in times of peace as war. Even their power has bounds prefcribed to it by a fuperior order, the voice of the people, whom they muft not prefume to oppofe. Befides, pleafures become infipid by being too familiar to them; and the fear and homage, with which men approach them, is an infurmountable obftacle to every connection of friendfhip. Good God, if private individuals could but cure themfelves of ambition and avarice, thofe mighty princes would foon be induced to envy the happinefs of their fubjects!

As to their riches, if they employ them as they ought, they would be fenfible, that they belong to the public, and not to themfelves; and, if they employ them
badly

badly, they will one day have a terrible account to settle with the great Judge. Their actions are cenfured and criticifed by all the world, and there is not even the humblest beggar, who does not think he has a right to enquire into their conduct. Let us pray to God for the prefervation of the good, and the converfion of the wicked, fuch being the duty of a Chriftian.

TALKATIVENESS.

IT has been obferved, that he who talks much, talks a great deal of nonfenfe, and therefore merits not the name of a wife man, fince he deprives every one in company of the ufe of their tongues. He often ftuns his auditors with his vociferous harangues, and at the fame time deprives himfelf of the power of thinking and properly digefting what he would fay. If he gives not himfelf leifure to digeft his thoughts, fo neither does he pay any regard to the choice of his words, but utters every thing crude and

and undigested. No wonder, if an harangue supported in this manner prove tedious and disgusting to all who hear it. He says every thing he believes, every thing he wishes, every thing he knows, and in order to furnish matter for the volubility of his tongue, he often says many things of which he is totally ignorant. He interlards his speech with so many useless observations, that the thread of his discourse is frequently lost; and he is not sensible of his error, till he at last finds himself left alone, one moving off after another.

LAWS.

LAWS were made by people of property and virtue, and afterwards accepted of by the people for the advantage of individuals. Prometheus was legislator of the Egyptians, Moses of the Jews, Solon of the Athenians, Lycurgus of the Lacedemonians, and Numa Pompilius of the Romans. Before those times men had no other laws than those
of

of nature, and the cuftoms introduced by their anceftors.

The intention of the legiflators was to weaken vice by the laws, and to give force and energy to juftice. Thefe intentions are no lefs laudable, than their effects are ufeful to the people, when the laws are executed with punctuality, and when neither the negligence of the fovereign, nor the corruption of the magiftrate, does not weaken them by injuftice.

The Greeks boafted of being a country of legiflators, the Romans made it their glory, that the laws were no where fo punctually obferved as among them; and the boaftings of the latter were perhaps better founded than thofe of the firft; for, of what confequence are laws, if they are not obferved? It is very true, that the Romans demanded of the Athenians the laws which Solon had formerly made, to extract from them what fuited their purpofe; but it is no lefs certain, that the Romans improved

I on

on thofe laws by an exact and rigorous obfervation of them.

I remember to have read in an old book, written by an Italian, * a very fingular matter relative to the laws of Athens, of which the Romans afked for a copy; and as I know of no other author who has fpoken of it but him, I fhall lay it before my readers as a curiofity.

He fays, that the Roman ambaffadors being arrived at Athens, and having explained the fubject of their deputation, the grand council affembled to deliberate whether they fhould agree with the requeft. After having examined the propofition, the judges refolved to fend to Rome a wife and fenfible man, to know whether the Romans were by their wifdom worthy of receiving the laws, which Solon had given to the people of Greece;

---

* *Specbio delle Scienze, par M. L. Fioravanti.*

Greece; but, if the ambaſſador found them rude and ignorant, he was to bring them back, without communicating them to the Romans.

This reſolution of the grand council of Athens could not be ſo concealed, but that the Romans got knowledge of it. The ſenate found themſelves very much embarraſſed, as at that time Rome was not provided with philoſophers capable of arguing with one of the wiſe men of Greece. The matter therefore to be conſidered, was by what means they ſhould get over this difficulty. The ſenate could think of no better method than to oppoſe a madman to the Greek philoſopher; and with this view, that if the madman ſhould happen by chance to prevail, the honour of Rome would be ſo much the more glorious, as a mad Roman would in that caſe confound a Grecian philoſopher; and, if the latter ſhould triumph, Athens could derive but little honour in boaſting of having cloſed the mouth of a madman at Rome.

The

The Athenian ambaſſador being arrived at Rome, he was led immediately to the capitol, and introduced into an apartment richly furniſhed, where was ſeated, in an elbow chair, a madman dreſſed in the habit of a ſenator, whom they had expreſsly ordered not to ſpeak a word. At the ſame time, the Grecian philoſopher was told, that the ſenator was very learned, but that he was a man of few words.

The Athenian was then introduced, and, without ſpeaking a word, lifted up one finger of his hand. The madman, ſuppoſing this was a threatning ſignal to pull out one of his eyes, and remembering that he was ordered not to ſpeak, lifted up three of his fingers, wiſhing to ſignify thereby, that if the Grecian ſhould put out one of his eyes, he would put out both his, and ſtrangle him with the third finger. The philoſopher, in lifting up one of his fingers, wiſhed to be underſtood, that there was but one ſupreme Being, who directed every thing; and believed,
that

The Madman and Grecian Philosopher.

that the three fingers the madman had
lifted up implied, that with God the paft,
prefent, and future, were the fame thing,
and from thence concluded that he, who
in fact was only a madman, was a great
philofopher.

The Grecian fage then held his hand
opened to the innocent man, meaning
thereby, that nothing is concealed from
God; but the madman, fuppofing this
to be a fign that he meant to give him a
flap on the face, clinched his fift faft, and
fhook it at the philofopher, wifhing him
thereby to underftand, that, if he executed
his threats, he would meet with a refolute
oppofition. The Greek, being already
prepoffeffed in favour of the madman,
conceived the meaning in a very different
light, and concluded in himfelf, that the
Romans meant, by a clinched fift, that
God comprifes all the univerfe in his
hand. Judging from thence of the profound wifdom of the Romans, he granted them without any further enquiry,

the

the laws of Solon, according to their request.

On the whole, laws are so necessary, and of so much consequence for the preservation of the people, that without them every thing would fall into a dreadful confusion.

FEASTS.

THERE is more ostentation and parade in great feasts than satisfaction. A great number of soups and ragouts, which should be eaten hot, as well as sauces, are almost cold before they reach the table; many unknown faces, and some of them often disagreeable, crowded so together as frequently not to give liberty to the arms to act; the inattention of servants, who, having too much to do, cannot serve every one, besides the whole hours, this pompous mode of eating occupies—certainly all these inconveniencies cannot be agreeable to a wise man, who wishes to be at ease.

Besides

Besides this, all the healths which are given, and which you must drink, though those persons may be as indifferent to you as the Great Mogul, serve only to drown the stomach, and to destroy all the powers of digestion. Add to all these, the great obligation you are under to the man, who furnishes you with all these elegant inconveniencies. Surely there can be nothing of this kind agreeable to people, who love peaceful and tranquil pleasures.

Experience tells us, that the true pleasures of the table consist in the good company of five or six friends, a few dishes well cooked, and served up hot. If any thing more be wanting, it can be only a little cheerful wine, and the liberty of drinking no more than we like.

A COUNTRY LIFE.

OF all the situations in which a man may find himself in this world, the country life is perhaps the sweetest and most agreeable. He who is born a gentleman, quietly enjoys the possessions of

of his anceftors, and lives in the country,
is generally void of ambition, and confequently is not tormented by the vain
defires of changing his condition, nor deceived by the falfe hopes of titles and dignities.

He confines his purfuits to the improve-
ment of his lands, and, when the year
proves favourable, he collects the rewards
of his cares, which is more agreeable to
him than the greateft revenue arifing from
any public place he might enjoy, which
every moment expofes him to envy, and
threatens him with a dreadful fall, or at
leaft with fome fatal reverfe of fortune.

He enjoys his little revenue in peace
and tranquillity, and his employments
are nothing more than an agreeable
amufement.   He truly poffeffes the
pleafures of life; for every feafon of the
year fupplies him with bufinefs, profit,
or paftime.   He fees no countenance
that difpleafes him, and he is free from
the neceffity of flattering or regaling the
proud, who are often unworthy of even
the

the moſt homely accommodation. He pays no court in the morning but to his fields, and his family ſupplies the place of aſſemblies at night.   Hunting ſerves him for a diverſion, and fiſhing for a profitable amuſement.   Age approaches him by pleaſing and gentle ſteps, and his life cloſes in peace and tranquillity.

HEALTH.

THE generality of men are ſo blind to themſelves, as to treat with the greateſt indifference, and the moſt trifling management, two important matters, to which they ought to pay their whole attention, and thoſe are their ſalvation and health.   The value of the firſt comprehends a happy or miſerable eternity, and the ſecond a life free from pain and grief ; for, without health, there can be no felicity.

The grandeurs, riches, and honours of this world, become taſtelefs and inſipid to the man who is deprived of the rich treaſures of health.   Nothing can afford
diverſion

diverfion to a fick man, and nothing can
confole him who labours under excru-
ciating pain. Every thing taftes difagreeable to a difordered palate, and the vale-
tudinarian cannot relifh even the choiceft
food.

When we confider the manner in which
the generality of mankind live, we are led
to conclude, that they take a great deal of
pains to make themfelves ill. They eat
without being hungry, they drink without
being dry, pafs whole nights without fleep-
ing, hover over the fire when they are not
cold, and do every thing they can to deprive
themfelves of the ineftimable bleffings of
health.

After having paffed the prime of their
days in this irregular manner, age rapidly
advances, accompanied with its ufual
infirmities, which are encreafed by the
imprudent conduct of their youthful
days. It is in this latter feafon of life,
that pain and grief begin, too late, to
make them fenfible of their paft errors.

They

They then in vain lament the irregular
conduct that has produced thefe evils,
and we cannot help pitying their folly
in having taken fo little care of their
health, which would, in fome meafure,
have contributed to foften the calamities
of old age. Though young people daily
fee proofs of this nature in perfons advanced in age, yet, notwithstanding thefe
living examples, the mind is fo blinded
by the paffions, that they pay not the
leaft regard to them. Oh! how imprudent is our youth! how grievous our old
age!

OLD AGE.

EVERY one wifhes to reach a good
old age, but few perfons wifh to be
thought old. The love of the vanities of
this world, and the fears of death, are
the caufe of the firft; and the imperfections which accompany age, and render
men a load to themfelves and others, are
the reafons for the fecond.

If

If we properly confider the fubject, we fhall readily conclude, that an honourable old age is the crown of a virtuous life, and that the white locks of an old man, free from reproach, are the laurels with which time has crowned him, and is an homage paid to his virtues. Every old man, who leads a life agreeable to his age, merits refpect, and the number of his years ought to be confidered as fo many fteps he has rifen above the follies of youth.

It fometimes however happens, that vice, though it generally quits us with age, ftill lurks in the heart of the old man, and gains fufficient influence to rekindle his paffions. We muft not then be aftonifhed, if fuch an old age, feparated from vir-tue, becomes the object of univerfal con-tempt.

VAIN GLORY.

VAIN-GLORY is a branch of pride, and a fin fo odious in the eyes of God, that Lucifer and his millions of angels

for

for having been guilty of it, were immediately punifhed, and precipitated into the bottomlefs pit. How many unhappy effects does vain-glory produce! It often prevents us from doing all the good we might, and frequently leads us to do that we ought to have fhunned.

We read in the Roman Hiftory, that the Conful Manilius one day afked Cæfar, what conduct he thought the moft proper to acquire true glory. " It is (replied he) to pardon injuries eafily, and largely to recompence thofe who ufe us well." Thefe were the fentiments of a Chriftian in the heart of a Pagan, which ought to make us afhamed of ourfelves, fince, notwithftanding we profefs Chriftianity, we commit worfe actions than a Pagan.

How many people do we not daily fee, who are totally averfe to forgiving an injury, equally through a motive of vain glory, as the fear of being confidered as a poltroon? How many others, to make an oftentation of their bravery, have entirely ftifled the virtue of charity

K   fo

-fo much recommended by the evangelifts?
How many do we not conftantly meet
with, who, through a principle of vain-
glory, have affected to follow all the
vices of the age, though their inclinations
were not naturally inclined that way?
How many alfo boaft of having committed
infamous actions, in order to pleafe thofe
with whom they were converfing?

We hardly ever meet with thofe men,
who make it their glory to relate the
virtuous actions they have performed.
Such is the extreme corruption of the age
in which we live, and fo incomprehenfible
is the folly of men, which carries them fo
far as to think, that they fhould fall fhort
in the number of their crimes, if they did
not make a glory of thofe they have already
committed.

FIDELITY.

A FAITHFUL friend is the re-
pofitory of our fecrets, and is like a
precious ftone which has no fpots, and
which is not to be purchafed but by

returns

returns of the fame nature.—Happy he who finds fuch a friend; for to him he can entruft his moft fecret thoughts, and in him find a confolation at all times.

Diodorus the Sicilian fays, that among the Egyptians it was a criminal matter to difcover a fecret with which they were entrufted; and one of their priefts, being convicted of this offence, was banifhed his country. Certainly nothing can be more juft, than that a fecret entrufted to a friend, under the fanction of good faith and fecrecy, fhould be confidered as a fa-cred thing, and that to divulge it, under any pretence whatever, is a profanation of the moft facred duties.

Plutarch remarks, that the Athenians, being at war with Philip, King of Mace-don, one day intercepted a letter, which he had written to Olympia his wife. They fent it back to him unopened, that they might not be obliged to read it in public, faying that their laws forbid them to be-tray a fecret.

The

The infidelity of a friend is certainly repugnant to nature itself, and that to betray a secret entrusted to us is truly deteſtable. A man who entruſts his ſecrets to another is like him, who ſurrenders his arms, and declares himſelf a ſlave; but how great would be the infamy of him, to whom we have ſurrendered them, were he to turn thoſe very arms againſt us, and aſſaſſinate us in that defenceleſs ſtate! Thus fidelity is the greateſt treaſure a man can find, and the ſecret entruſted to him the higheſt mark of ſincere friend-ſhip.

SINGULARITY.

A MAN of ſingularity is a very diſagreeable character, ſince he pleaſes nobody, and is every moment drawing on himſelf enemies almoſt without his perceiving it. Singularity is the conſequence of a concealed preſumption, which ſeeks to make itſelf admired by ſentiments and manners totally contrary to the notions of others, and

to

to appear brilliant by an extraordinary
tafte for things. The man who is of this
ftamp, difcovers no wit in what other people fay, nor fees any thing pleafing in
what others delight. He endeavours to
raife himfelf above human nature by opinions contrary to all the reft of the world,
and thereby falls into univerfal hatred and
contempt.

There feems to be an antipathy between the fingular man and all the reft of
the world; for every perfon of good
fenfe and found judgment cautioufly fhun
him. He efteems nothing but what he
poffeffes, or what comes from himfelf,
and finds neither worth nor merit in what
others poffefs, or in any thing they do.
He is a true copy of Momus, for he
has fomething to fay againft every one.
Nature feems to have formed fuch a man
for folitude, for he is of no value in the
commerce of human nature. He, who
cannot accommodate himfelf to the humour of others, will never be efteemed
nor loved.

FALSE

FALSE PRAISE.

THE habit of praising every thing we fee, and every thing we hear, is a mark of a weak judgment, or the fign of a falfe heart. He who applauds every thing wifhes to pleafe all the world, not reflecting at the fame time, that he who praifes only with a view to make his court to others, fuffers his judgment to become a dupe to his complaifance.

It is truly the character of a coxcomb to admire every thing he fees or hears; and there is but little fatisfaction in being worfhipped by any one, who erects altars to all forts of idols. Such a man conftantly expofes himfelf to be repaid with ingratitude, fince no one pays any regard to fuch affected complaifance. By fuch a conduct, he leads every one to fuppofe, that he finds beauty in deformity, wit in nonfenfe, wifdom in ignorance, bravery in cowardice, modefty in impudence, prudence in avarice, generofity in prodigality, and virtue in vice. He himfelf
muft

muſt be convinced, that he wants either judgment or probity.

PHILOSOPHY.

PHILOSOPHY is the mother of the ſciences, and diſpoſes men to accommodate themſelves to every condition of human life; for it is by the aſſiſtance of Philoſophy that we arrive at the knowledge of every thing. True Philoſophy is known by the contempt it teaches for all terreſtrial things, and by not ſubmitting its ſpirit to the cares and anxieties, which accompany the vanities of this world.

The true Philoſopher knows leſs of the malice of this world, than of the courſe of the ſtars; and finds more pleaſure and advantage in not knowing evil, than in comprehending the ebbing and flowing of the ſea. The Philoſopher Anacharſis, one day, among other things, thus wrote to Crœſus: "Know, Crœſus, that the Athenian academy does not teach us to command, but to be commanded and to obey; not to ſay much, but rather

to

to learn to be filent; not to revenge, but rather to pardon; not to covet the poffeffions of others, but to give part of our own to the needy; not to feek after honours, but to cultivate virtue; and not to be eager in the purfuit of much, but to be contented with a little.

In this only confifts true Philofophy; all the reft is but bafe coin and tinfel.

The firft Philofopher, of whom we have any celebrated account, was Thales, who, on account of his virtues and great merit, was placed at the head of the feven wife men of Greece, though he was not by birth a Grecian, being originally of Miletes in Afia. It is faid, that he was the firft who acknowledged the immortality of the foul, who invented aftronomy, difcovered the caufe of eclipfes, &c. Since his time, there have appeared a number of Philofophers. who much more merit the epithet of Buffoons of Parnaffus, than of being confidered as its ornaments. So dangerous it is to affect great characters.

Among

Among the philofophers, who made the moft fplendid figure after Thales, were the five following.

Pythagoras was the chief of that fect, which, after his name, were called Pythagoreans, whofe difciples were obliged to obferve a profound filence of five years, before they could be admitted as a proficient in that fect. It has with propriety been doubted, whether any Frenchman could ever be one of this fraternity.

The fecond was Plato, furnamed the *divine*, the chief of the Academicians, fo named from the place where he taught being called the Academy. He lived to the age of eighty-one years, which is, in fome meafure, attributed to the moderation his philofophy taught.

The third was Ariftotle, the chief of the Peripatetics. He was a difciple of Plato, and taught as he walked.

The fourth was Zeno. He taught in a place called Stoa, and from thence the fect was called Stoics. Among all
the

the Pagan Philofophers, his morals were the moft pure, and approached the neareft to thofe of Chriftianity. He taught his pupils to be regardlefs of grief, to pay no attention to the fufferings of the body, to treat riches with contempt, and to beftow all their time in the purfuit of wifdom and virtue. St. Paul, before his converfion to Chriftianity, was of this fect.

The fifth was Epicurus, who was faid to allow of every kind of enjoyment and voluptuoufnefs; though there are others, who reprefent his doctrines in a different light. After all, the trueft philofophy is properly to know ourfelves, and to live in fuch a manner in this world as may fecure us a happy eternity.

THINK BEFORE YOU ACT.

THE little reflection men make before they undertake any thing, is the natural confequence of their fo often repenting of what they have done. A precipitate refolution is frequently the forerunner
of

of an unfortunate finifh. If a man, in order to make a public difcourfe, employs fometimes whole days in compofing it, with how much more reafon ought he to take a long time to confider, when he is to determine on a matter, on which his honour, repofe, and fortune, may materially depend!

Demetrius, the fon of the great Antigonus, one day replied to Patrocles his general, who expreffed his impatience to give the enemy battle, " Remember, Patrocles, that it is of little ufe to reflect on a mifcarriage, which an imprudent hafte may occafion; we ought firft maturely to confider the matter, and then conclude with judgment." Suetonius faid, that Auguftus was a long time in forming his friendfhips, but having orce contracted them, he was firm ard unfhaken. Plutarch, in his life of Pertorius, pays him great compliments; faying, that he was very flow to determine, but afterwards very firm in his refolutions. Such a character is worthy

of

of a great man; for whatever may be said
of certain occaſions, in which a ſudden reſolution may be beſt, and where the leaſt
delay would be dangerous, yet, if preci-
pitation in deſign, and ſlowneſs in execution, ſometimes produce happy events,
it may be compared to a lottery, in which
there are an hundred blanks to one
prize.   Every thing in nature advances
ſlowly, and is long arriving at ma-
turity.

VIRTUE.

VIRTUE is the daughter of Heaven;
happy thoſe who cultivate it from their infancy; they paſs their youth in ſerenity,
their manhood in tranquillity, and their
old age without remorſe.   There is nothing
in this world fit to be compared with it; all
its wiſhes and deſires tend to celeſtial enjoyments, which are not liable to change.   The
virtuous man looks back on his paſt
conduct without regret, becauſe his time
has been well employed; and has no
apprehenſions

apprehenfions for the future, becaufe his fate cannot but be happy. His mind is the feat of cheerfulnefs, and his actions are the foundations of felicity; he is rich amidft poverty; and no one can deprive him of what he poffeffes; he is all perfection, for his life is fpotlefs; and he has nothing to wifh for, fince he poffeffes every thing. Alexander was celebrated for his courage, Ptolemy for his learning, Trajan for his love of truth, Antonius for his piety, Conftantius for his temperance, Scipio for his continence, and Theodofius for his humility. O glorious virtue, which, in fome way or other rewards all its admirers, and without whom there can be no real happinefs!

LIBERTY.

OF all the vanities of this world, liberty is the moft precious, and nature has kindly favoured us with this treafure to foften the ills of life. All the world admire it, but few know how properly to preferve it. Avarice and ambition are

L   its

its greateſt enemies, and the moſt capable
of engaging men to pay homage at the
ſhrine of ſlavery.

That men ſhould ſacrifice their liberty
to court the favour of the great is truly
wonderful, yet not ſmall is the number
of thoſe who worſhip the Idol of Fortune.
To part with our liberty merely to obtain
the favours or the ſmiles of the rich and
powerful, is buying wretchedneſs and
miſery at a great price. Such a man re-
ſembles the moth, who flutters round the
flame of a candle, to enjoy the light it
emits, till it burns its wings, becomes
crippled, and can fly no longer.

Happy the man who can eat when he
pleaſes, ſleep as long as he likes, and
go wherever his inclination carries him.
There is ſomething ſo ſweet in liberty,
that we plainly ſee the love of it predominant in animals, ſome of whom die in
confinement. But the worſt ſpecies of
ſlavery is that condition, which reduces
a man to the abject ſtate of being obliged
to ſay and act, without regard to the

diĉtates

dictates of truth, or confcience, what fome
rich tyrant fhall pleafe to direct him.
Preferable to fuch a fituation is the abode
of plague, peftilence, and famine.

DEPENDANCE.

IT is generally faid, " Happy is he
who depends on no one but himfelf;"
but where are we to find that perfon?
Such is the condition of human beings,
that there is no ftate independant, from
the fceptre to the fhepherd's crook.
The greatnefs of the fovereign depends
on the obedience of his fubjects, and the
good or bad condition of the fubjects on
the wifdom or weaknefs of the Prince.
The buffoon of Philip II. King of Spain,
one day faid to that Prince, " What
would you do, Philip, if your fubjects
fhould take it into their heads to fay *no*,
every time that you faid *yes?*"   A reflection replete with wifdom, and worthy of
the wifeft man.

Thus the great depend on the little,
and the little on the great; the valet on

his

his mafter, and the mafter on his valet;
the avaricious man on his money, and
the proud man on his folly; the luxurious man on vice, and the felicity of
this world on the imagination; the na-
tional expences on the revenues, and the
revenues on the labour of the fubject;
navigation on favourable winds, and war
on fortune; true happinefs on a good
confcience, and this on a life without reproach.

Even the elements are not independent,
fince they cannot fubfift without the mutual affiftance of each other. The animals depend on the earth, from which
they draw their fubfiftance, and the earth
depends on good feafons, without which
it can produce neither fruits nor vegetables; the rain depends on the clouds, and
the clouds on the vapours of the earth,
and all together depend on the Divine
direction. God alone being abfolutely
independent, it is he who has created all
things with a mutual dependance upon
each

each other, in order to make us fenfible of our imperfections, and that nothing is perfect, except the Creator of all things.

SPEECH.

EVERY man, who is not dumb, fpeaks; but every one who fpeaks has not the art of pleafing: to be capable of doing that, genius, judgment, and rhetoric, are neceffary. To fpeak properly is certainly a great accomplifhment, and there are few acquifitions that are to be compared to it; for though words are nothing but founds that ftrike the ear, they have neverthelefs fo much force, that the life or death of a man is often determined by them.

We read in Jofephus's Hiftory of the Jews, that after the death of Marc Anthony, (the competitor of Auguftus) Herod, King of the Jews, and a great partifan of Anthony, took the refolution to prefent himfelf to Auguftus; and, placing

L 3

his

his crown at his feet, he accompanied his submiffion with fo eloquent an harangue, that Auguftus found himfelf forced, not only to reftore him his crown, but alfo to introduce him to a number of his moft intimate friends.

Pyrrhus, king of Epire, was a generous and magnanimous prince, a good foldier, liberal, and admirably patient under a reverfe of fortune, but more particularly famous for his fweetnefs of temper, being befides endowed with fuch perfuafive and infinuating eloquence, as gave the higheft pleafure and delight to all who heard him, upon whatever fuhject he fpoke. It was for this reafon that the Roman fenate, having fent Ambaffadors to him, forbade them to treat with him immediately, but to wait till the fecond or third interview, fearing that by his eloquence he might draw them over to his party.

Plato faid, that by the words of a man, we learn to difcover thofe internal faculties, which we cannot fee. Titus Livius,

Livius, Diodorus, Pliny, Plato, Plutarch, and many other authors, always fpoke in high commendation of the eloquence of the Greek and Latin princes, who raifed themfelves to the higheft employment, rather by their genius and eloquence, than by victories and an illuftrious birth. ·

· Antoninus, furnamed the Pious, in giving his daughter Fauftina to Marcus Aurelius, who had nothing to boaft of but philofophy, he faid, he would much rather have for a fon-in-law a wife poor man, than a foolifh prince. Laftly, fpeech places the real diftinction between men, and difcovers their capacity, excufes their defects, and raifes their merit. Happy thofe who can fpeak well, or know how properly to be filent.

SILENCE.

SILENCE may be the effects of wifdom or ftupidity. He muft be a very difagreeable companion, who fays nothing, becaufe he knows nothing; he is, however,

ever, far preferable to the man, who speaks a great deal, and says nothing to the purpose. The silence of a wise man is a proof of solid speculation; and such a man, if he speak little, he generally carries conviction with him when he does speak. The philosopher Xenocrates, being one day at a feast, was asked, why he talked so little. He replied, he had often repented of speaking too much, but never of saying too little.

It is said of Demosthenes, who was a great orator, and a philosopher of an exemplary life, that, amidst all his good qualities, he was addicted to talking too much, which induced the Athenian assembly to assign him a pension, not with a view that he might teach philosophy, but that he might have occasion to talk less.

To be a disciple of Pythagoras, the first qualification necessary was to keep silence for five years, as we have before observed. The end of this philosophy was undoubtedly to make a man master
of

of his tongue, which certainly is a very neceffary knowledge. " Confine your tongue, (fays the old proverb) or your tongue will confine you."

Hence filence may be confidered as a mark of ftupidity in fome perfons, and of good fenfe in others. It is certain, that in the affairs of the ftate cabinet, filence is effential; in thofe of love it is neceffary; and, in particular affairs, filence is very often ufeful, fince, by fpeaking too much, the moft important fecrets may efcape us. In fhort, filence in a wife man is a venerable modefty, and, in a fool, is a favour done to fociety.

SELF-LOVE.

SELF-LOVE is the general defect of human nature, and the moft dangerous enemy of reafon. It is the groundwork of the greater part of our crimes, and the favourite of our natural inclinations. It is that which fans the flame
of

of pride, makes avarice infatiable, tickles the luxurious, warms the bilious, feeds the glutton, and lulls the idle to fleep.

It commands the helm of all human actions, and banifhes 'every' reflection that oppofes the tyranny of its will. It is the moft dangerous enemy we have, and is the more difficult to conquer, as it has the fecret of perfuading us, that it propofes nothing but what is for our own intereft.

If we candidly examine all our actions, we fhall foon be convinced, that felf-love is our reigning principle. Do we pretend to love any particular perfon? It is ourfelves we love in that perfon. Do we hate any one? Self-love is at the bottom of it. Self-love, however, is in fome inftances neceffary, fince, without fome attention to it, we might become the dupes of the artful and defigning; and though it is abfolutely neceffary we fhould keep felf-love within due bounds, yet it would not be prudent entirely to deftroy it.

TEARS.

TEARS.

TEARS are the muficians of Sorrow and Defpair, they are the echo of the -doleful lamentations of the afflicted, and a bitter paftime to thofe who are obliged to fhed them. 'There appear to be five different forts of tears: the firft are of *forrow*, the fecond thofe of *joy*, the third of *rage*, the fourth of *love*, and the fifth thofe of *penitence*.

As to the firft fort of tears, they are juft, and even becoming, when they are fhed with moderation on the death of a parent or friend; but, when let fall on any other account, fuch as the lofs of earthly poffeffions, or any other uneafinefs caufed by fuch-like motives, they are certainly very badly employed.

Thofe tears, which we fometimes fee people let fall on the firft meeting, after a long abfence, of a dear and particular friend, are the fure figns of a tender and

and sincere affection; and may be regarded as sacrifices which sorrow makes to joy, and which may be considered as the overflowings of a noble and generous -heart.

The third sort of tears are composed of venomous drops, which rage produces, and mark the excess of fury, which is disappointed of taking its revenge in the manner it wishes.

The fourth kind of tears are the most foolish and ridiculous of all, I mean those of lovers. But these are too ridiculous to dwell on.

The fifth kind of tears are those of penitence, which will one day shine in the crown of glory, with which God shall hereafter reward them. The tears of repentance lead to the paths of happiness.

IMPERFECTIONS OF HUMAN NATURE.

NO mortal is so perfect as to be totally free from vice, nor any person so vicious as not to possess some virtue.

The

The ancient authors have accufed Homer of vanity, Alexander of madnefs, Cæfar of ambition, Pompey of pride, Hannibal of perfidy, Vefpafian of avarice, Trajan of violence, and Marc Anthony of luxury. Thus, among all the famous princes, not one is to be found, whofe character does not afford a mixture of virtues and vices. It has been obferved in all ages, that the greateft men have generally had the greateft vices. Nature feems to have placed a fpot in fome particular part of all her works: let us not therefore attempt to reform the weakneffes of others from our own feeble reafonings, but admire the good qualities of every one, and have pity on their defects, fince we ourfelves are in want of the fame degree of charity.

The Impoffibility of pleafing every one.

IT is impoffible for any man to pleafe all the world, fince one loves what another hates, and what one efteems, another defpifes. Generally fpeaking,

M   he

he who attempts to pleafe every body, generally pleafes no one; for, in order to be
pleafing to every one, he muſt ſhew his approbation of conducts as different from
each other, as light is from darkneſs; ſo
that his deceitful complaifance being once
known, he draws on himſelf contempt, in-
ſtead of eſteem.

A wife man cannot pleafe a fool, and,
as the world abounds with fools, the
number we may pleafe can be but ſmall.
If the wife man, with all the brilliancy
of his virtue, cannot acquire univerfal
approbation, how can the fool be expected
to obtain it? It is extreme vanity in any
man to imagine he can pleafe all the
world. Every man, who knows his own
imperfections, will never flatter himfelf
with being able to pleafe many people.—
This knowledge of himfelf will produce
indifference, and that indifference will
place him much more at his eafe, and he
will enjoy more profound tranquillity,
than the man who aims at univerfal
approbation, and who will at laſt find,
that

that he has been purfuing but a fha-pow.

The ambition we have of pleafing all the world comes from the good opinion we have of ourfelves, and this ferves to flatter us with the hopes of fuccefs, till experience convinces us, that we are giving ourfelves much trouble in the purfuit of what we fhall never overtake.—Let us live honeftly, and free from the reproach of our own confciences, without caring about the approbation of the greateft part of mankind, who generally judge of others by their own inclinations or averfions.

INTERFERENCE.

THE man, who unneceffarily interferes in the concerns of others, often finds himfelf embarked on a boifterous ocean. A certain philofopher ufed to fay, that he would much rather be a judge in the caufe between two of his enemies, than between two of his friends; for, of the firft, he fhould at leaft make one friend; whereas, of the laſt, he ſhould probably loſe one; that is, the perſon againſt whom he gave his opinion.

The beſt method is certainly to ſtand neuter in affairs, in which we have any perſonal intereſt. Beſides, thoſe who are fond of meddling with the affairs of others, are generally people of a reſtleſs and bad diſpoſition, ſince they find pleaſure in intermixing in broils and quarrels. It has been obſerved, that people of a quarrelſome and litigious character have generally no friends; for, being accuſtomed to blow the coals of contention, which Chriſtian charity tells us we ought not to do, but, as far as lies in our power, endeavour to extinguiſh the flame, they draw on themſelves the contempt and averſion of every honeſt perſon.

By endeavouring to ſeparate two vagabonds who are fighting, we frequently expoſe ourſelves to the danger of receiving ſome marks of their brutality.—The ſame thing happens to him, who

interferes

interferes in matters with which he has no reafon to meddle. I faw an inftance of this nature at Amfterdam, in the perfon of a native of Bruffels, who offered himfelf as a fecond to a German gentleman, of whom he knew nothing, and merely becaufe he had heard that the gentleman had an affair of honour with another perfon, with whom he was equally unacquainted. Being arrived at the fpot where the affair was to be fettled, fword in hand, this bufy and meddle-making man made ufe of fo many injurious expreffions to the fecond of the oppofite parry, as obliged him, being a man of honour and fpirit, to draw his fword, when, on the firft onfet, he laid the aggreffor dead on the fpot, to the entire fatisfaction of all prefent. Thus the principal actors in this fcene were prevented from finifhing their affair, and were fatisfied with one fool having loft his life. Such was the confequence of his idle interference.

COMPANIES.

A MAN is generally said to be known by the company he keeps.—Ravens are generally seen among dead carcases, and bees among flowers. There is nothing of more consequence to a young man than to chuse such company as may do him credit, and from whom he may take the model of his conduct and manners.— The mind of man is so formed, that it copies what is before it, without thinking, whether it be good or bad. We must keep at a distance from every thing that can stain the morals, treat all the world with civility, but cautiously keep from the company of those who are capable of giving bad examples.

The practice of these precautions is very difficult for young people to attend to, whose strong and impetuous passions, having nothing in view but to satisfy themselves, eagerly embrace the company of those who humour their whims and caprice, Many instances are frequently produced of
young

young people, who, while under the guidance of their parents or friends, have given the moſt promiſing Hopes of a wiſe and prudent conduct; but no ſooner were they become maſters of themſelves, and having had the misfortune to fall into the company of profligates, than, in imitation of them, they ran into all their vices, and at laſt periſhed miſerably. Every one, who deſpiſes this advice in his youth, will not fail to be ſenſible of his error when it may perhaps be too late, and when it muſt infallibly be ſucceeded by deſpair, horror, and remorſe. It is a melancholy ſtate indeed, when we arrive at the borders of old age, to find no hope is left us but in ſorrow and repentance.

COMPASSION.

THERE are two ſorts of men who are incapable of compaſſion. The firſt are the great and rich, who, being ignorant of what want and oppreſſion are, cannot be ſo ſenſible of miſery as they ought. The

ſecond

second sort are those, who, being naturally hard-hearted, are insensible to the misfortunes of their neighbours. The first would be in some measure excusable, were they ignorant of the divine precepts, which the sacred writings hold forth to them concerning universal charity ; but the second sort are totally inexcusable, since it is through cruelty and malice that they look with consummate indifference on the miseries of others.

The rich and powerful are obliged to acquire this virtue, because here on earth they hold the place of him, whose pity and compassion they will one day stand so much in need of themselves, and who will measure out to them his mercy and pity, in proportion as they have bestowed it on others. But that unfeeling set of men, who have a heart insensible of pity and compassion, would do well to read those dreadful judgments, which the scriptures denounce against them.

Though every age produces unfeeling and obdurate hearts, and compassion exists
generally

generally more in words than actions, yet we meet with some noble and generous souls, who most sensibly feel for the misfortunes of others, and take the greatest pleasure in alleviating their sorrows, and assisting them in their necessities. After all, however, happy are those, who are not in want of compassion. It is an old proverb, it is better to be envied that pitied.

SINCERITY.

SINCERITY is the mother of Truth, and the ensign of an honest man; it is the pledge of our words, and the picture of our thoughts. There is no need of vouchers for the truth of what it says, and its protestations are indisputable. It encloses several virtues in itself, for it never deceives or flatters any one. Its promises are considered as matters already done, and its protestations are sacred records. An openness of heart is its device, and it has no other end in view but honour. It does not deceive by
appearance,

appearance, for it is in itfelf plain and
fimple; it is a ftranger to falfity, fince it
fpeaks nothing but truth; it every where
makes itfelf known, and never wifhes to be
concealed; it fears no enemies, for virtue
is its friend; it is held in efteem by every
honeft perfon, though privately defpifed
by the bafe and treacherous; it is
banifhed from courts, and is unknown
among the rich and dignified; its birth
is in the heart, and its abode on the lips.
It feems as if it had abandoned the earth,
fince malignity has found the fecret of
making it pafs for ftupidity among the
greater part of men. For my own part,
I believe it has taken its flight to heaven,
that it may no longer be witnefs of the
triumphs of Falfity and Deceit.

PROMISES.

THE facility of making promifes,
and the difficulty of performing them,
are almoft fimilar. It is a folly to ruin
ourfelves by promifes, and it is a meannefs
to enrich ourfelves by avoiding the
performance

performance. An old proverb fays, " Promifes are females, and the performance of them males; fince we fee more of the firft than of the laft."

It is generally obferved, that thofe who are the moft ready to promife are generally thofe who are the leaft in condition to fulfil their promifes. It is a very great imprudence to make promifes in order to gain friends for a little time, and afterwards to make them our enemies by thinking no more of what we faid. It feems to me, that it is infinitely better to oblige without promifing, than to bemean ourfelves by promifing without effect. The fool makes engagements with all the world without the leaft difcrimination; but the wife man obliges only thofe who deferve it. The man, who readily offers his purfe to another who he knows will not accept of it, will not, when afked, lend any man a half-penny. Indeed, I hold great promifes in fo little efteem, that the inftant they are made me, I would

very

very willingly give them up for the least reality.

RANK.

THE pride of rank or title is certainly one step beneath the other follies of this world. It seems to be the completion of human vanity and impertinence, to consider it as a necessary point, to take the first seat at a sumptuous entertainment, merely from the consideration of being possessed of a title. The elbow-chair or the stool will equally display merit; and he, who occupies the latter, may probably have more sense and discernment, than he who lolls at his ease in the first. The man, who is not seated at table, according to his rank, generally enjoys little comfort of his dinner. What folly! Is the soup better, when placed where his vanity wishes to have a seat, than at any other part of the table? Is it reasonable for a man to lose his appetite, because he is seated one chair lower than he thinks his dignity merits? should he

wish

wifh to be ferved firft at table, that would
be pardonable, provided he was more
hungry than others; but, if it be only
from the confideration of his rank, that
he has confequently more merit than the
reft of the company, and that greater
attention ought to be paid him on that
account, it is the higheft mark of impertinence, and renders him unworthy of
the loweft feat. A coxcomb, prepoffeffed
with this imagination, wifhes the mafter
of the houfe to prefent him with the
firft glafs of wine, without confidering
who may be in the moft want of it.
This folly of rank is carried to fuch a
height and degree of infolence, that it
has even crept into the churches, where
the dignified man cannot pray to his God
but in the moft confpicuous and elegant
feat. Laftly, people, who are in love
with their rank and title, are very tire-
fome animals, fworn enemies to the
pleafure of others, and efpecially to the
conviviality of the table, where the
liberty and eafe of the company ought
N not

not to be reftrained by any perfonal dif-
tinctions.

THE SPIRIT OF CONTRADICTION.

THE man who knows the leaft, generally fpeaking, is he who takes the moft
pleafure in contradicting. His only refource being in the power of his lungs,
he ftuns his auditors with the loudnefs of
his words, and makes himfelf equally
odious to thofe whom he attacks, and
thofe who are obliged to endure the
tempeft of his voice. What a foolifh
character is that of the contradictor!
What pains does he not take to fhew his
ignorance, by talking of thofe things, of
which he knows nothing! Is it not a
fupreme degree of effrontery, for a man
to fet himfelf up as a judge of a difcourfe,
of which he perhaps does not know any
thing. Though contradiction, properly
timed, may fometimes furnifh matter for
converfation; yet, when it is accompanied
with obftinacy, it will foon become difgufting. To tire this fort of difagreeable
·2   difpofitions,

difpofitions, the beft is to give them their way in whatever they advance, when they will foon get tired, having no longer any thing to feed their nonfenfe. It has been faid of a certain nobleman, that he is very angry on being contradicted, and yet looks upon that man as a fool, who has not fomething to fay in oppofition to whatever is advanced. This kind of character is very difgufting, efpecially when they are mafters of fubtle argument. It is therefore beft, whenever we can, to avoid fuch company; and, when we cannot, we muft follow the advice of the old proverb, which fays, " Give hay to the ox, and grains to the fwine."

CONVENIENCE.

THAT conveniency, which mortals feek with fo much avidity in the courfe of this fhort life, appears to be a kind of fweet poifon, which fills the human mind with vanity, and is ranked among the greateft felicities of this world.

Conveniency, by which is meant the poffeffion of things agreeable to our wifhes, is the falfe friend of the body, and, under the pretence of making us happy, loads us with many evils. It deftroys induftry and exercife fo neceffary to the body, as it furnifhes us with all the dangerous delicacies of the table. Befides this, it lulls the foul into a ftate of lethargy, and too often makes us forget our God.

It is very difficult for the man, who is entirely at his eafe, to facrifice any pleafure to his health. The generality of men will not give themfelves leifure to recollect, that they cannot ferve two oppofite mafters at the fame time, and that it is impoffible to give way to all the vanities of this life, and at the fame time think of our duty to God and ourfelves.

The end of moft of our defires is to procure an agreeable independence for our old age, that we may live at eafe when we fhall be nearly verging on the borders
of

of the grave. Every one dreads the idea of wanting conveniences in that ftage of life, without confidering, that the greater part of mankind do not live to arrive at the age of fifty. A great part of what we call conveniences are little better than vices, for which we fhall be called to an account hereafter. A convenience is, in fome degree, properly called the gift of Heaven, provided we make a right ufe of it; for, improperly ufed, it becomes a curfe. The Scripture tells us, that Lazarus, labouring under the moft terrible infirmities of human nature during his life, on his quitting this world, was conveyed to the regions of eternal felicity; while the rich man, who here enjoyed all the luxuries of this life, was faid to have little comfort in the world above. This furely merits a moment's refleAion!

COMPLAISANCE.

COMPLAISANCE is the daughter of Civility, which eafily infinuates man-

kind

kind into the esteem of each other, and often forces people naturally of a savage disposition to be kind and civil. Every one is fond of the company of the complaisant man, because his conversation is at all times agreeable.

He seems to sympathize with every one with whom he converses, and consequently is pleasing to every one. Complaisance proves a knowledge of human life, and is the certain proof of a polite education. It distinguishes a man, without exposing him to envy; for even the envious are pleased with his obliging manners. Upon the whole, it is a character advantageous to every one.

After all, however estimable complaisance may be, the excess of it is good for nothing, unless it be to draw contempt on the over-complaisant man, or to make him pass for a dupe. Hence it seems that complaisance should not be left to itself, but always accompanied with judgment and prudence, without which it loses its merit, and exposes us to the mockery of others.

OATIIS.

OATHS.

EVERY fin has some pretended appearance of fatisfaction or pleafure, except the vice of fwearing. It is not only offenfive to God, but leffens the veracity of what the fwearer tells you, it being an old faying, that thofe who fwear will falfify. A man of credit and veracity has no occafion to call in the affiftance of oaths to make himfelf believed, fince he knows, that if his character has not weight enough to make his affertions believed, it is not oaths that will contribute to give them weight.

The man who is much given to fwearing, is generally guilty of many other vices; they are generally unfortunate in the world, and finifh their lives miferably. It is a very wicked cuftom to be every moment calling God to witnefs what they frequently know, at the very moment they are fpeaking, to be totally falfe. We have been told of a man, who had the misfortune to be a great fwearer, and who, being

being reprimanded by his confeſſor to no purpoſe, was at laſt enjoined, by way of penitence, to have a button pulled off his coat every time he ſwore; ſo that, at the end of twenty-four hours, he had not a coat left to wear. He now began to reflect, that, in a little time, he ſhould be obliged to have his clothes new-buttoned every day; and this bringing him to reflection, he at laſt happily broke himſelf of the habit of ſwearing.

THE RIDICULE OF BAD FORTUNE.

IT ſeems ás if mockery and ridicule were a tribute which the world pay to bad fortune, and that, to laugh at people ill-treated by that blind divinity, were a prerogative which thoſe in eaſy circumſtances had a right to indulge themſelves in. But ſurely nothing can be more ungenerous, than for one man to make a mockery of another, merely becauſe he may not have been ſo fortunate as himſelf. It is a great mark of pride and vanity,

vanity, and, in some measure, is a proof of the depravity of the heart. Those who act on this ungenerous principle would do well to recollect, that the gifts of fortune are fickle, and that some accident or other, in the commerce of human life, whatever may be our possessions at present, may strip us of them all, and place us in the very situation of those, with whom we have been so ungenerously free, as to turn them into ridicule for what they probably could not help, and which was owing to some unforeseen accident. Could we but be brought to think and act by others, in the same manner as we ourselves would wish to be done by, we should not mock the unfortunate man, but endeavour to console and assist him. To rejoice in the distresses of another is cruel to the last degree; for if we do not choose to relieve them, we have certainly no right to add to the load of their afflictions.

PRE-

PRESERVATION OF HEALTH.

OUR principal employment in youth is to difcover new pleafures, and in old age we are equally employed in the purfuit of what will eafe our pains, and preferve the little health we have left. It is with the view of leffening thefe cares, that I am now going to make fome few remarks, the obfervation of which may contribute to foften the infirmities of old age.

The firft rule is, to fhun thofe places where the air is thick and moift, and where violent winds are frequent; to keep the head, ftomach, and feet always warm, and to guard as much as poffible from the nocturnal air, which is very prejudicial to the health.

The fecond rule confifts in eating only when you are hungry, and not drinking but when you are dry, nor committing any excefs with either. To abftain from eating different forts of provifions at one time, and always to rife from table with

an

an appetite; never to eat at night, at moſt but a light ſupper; to faſt every tenth day, in order to give nature a reſt, and never to drink between meals, nor after midnight.

The third rule is, to go to bed in good hours, and riſe early in the morning, for ſeven hours ſleep is ſufficient for the re-poſe of a man; a longer time is hurtful to his health. Never ſleep after dinner; but, if that cannot be prevented, let it be only in an elbow chair, and that only for half an hour at moſt. Never uſe exerciſe of body or mind immediately after a meal, it being then as hurtful as it is uſe-ful at other times; and though exerciſe, according to Hippocrates, may be the ſureſt means of preſerving health, never-theleſs we muſt not puſh it ſo far as to fatigue us too much.

The fourth rule is, to have nothing to do with phyſicians, except in deſperate caſes, but to apply to the moſt ſimple and eaſy medicines, whenever nature requires ſome aſſiſtance.

The

The fifth is, to ufe pleafure with a moderation which will not tire in the enjoyment, and without fuffering ourfelves to be hurried away into excefs; in a word, to enjoy pleafure, but not to fuffer it to take poffeffion of us.

The fixth and laft rule is, not to fuffer ourfelves to be too much dejected on the mifcarriages of this life; for there is a very clofe connection between the body and the mind, fo clofe indeed, that the one cannot fuffer without difturbing the economy of the other.

Were people to obferve thefe rules, we fhould not fee fo many broken conftitutions in the early part of life; but unfortunately fuch is the difpofition of mankind, that they know not the value of health till after they have loft it, and do not think of confulting the difciples of Efculapius till after Bacchus and Venus have made irreparable breaches in their conftitutions.

REPOSE.

REPOSE.

THE wife man knows the value of repofe, but happy is he who actually enjoys it. It is the moft reafonable object of our wifhes, after having been difcouraged in the purfuits of our youth, and difappointed in the enjoyment of the tumultuous pleafures of this life; for it is only in repofe we can hope to reft in the evening of life. In order to obtain that pleafing fituation, we muft remove ourfelves far from every thing that can difturb our tranquillity, and abfolutely renounce, and never more to think of, what the world calls fortune, upon which we muft turn our backs, before we can boaft of happinefs; for, all things properly confidered, there can be neither grandeur, riches, nor honours, without inquietude. Hence the favours of fortune cannot be efteemed as promoting happinefs; and he, who lives in repofe in fome peaceful retreat, better enjoys the fweets of life undifturbed,

O than

than thofe who imagine they find every
felicity in the buftle of parade and grandeur.

Mainard, the French poet, has very
prettily defcribed the fituation of life to
be wifhed for. " Liften, my fon, (fays
he) to what forms the compofition of a
happy life.—Neither care nor law-fuit ;
a fufficiency of wealth, without the
trouble of labouring to procure it ;
friends, of an even temper, to converfe
with ; a found body, always neatly
dreffed, without finery ; no quarrels,
and provifions plaiñ and natural ; a mo-
deft good-tempered woman to affift in
domeftic matters, and a little fleep, but
that peaceful and tranquil, Be fatisfied
with fuch a lot, you having no room to
complain of it ; and you will then view
the approach of death without fear or defire."

Herein really confifts the true fortune
of this world ; but ambition and avarice
conceal it from the eyes of the generality
of mankind. Age, to which wifdom is
generally

generally confined, eafily difcovers this truth ; for having, in youth, experienced the vanity of the paffions, he cannot but defpife them, and look forward to repofe, as the only end of all his defires.

We read in hiftory, that Plato, Marcius, Cato, Lucullus, Scipio, Pericles, Seneca, and Dioclefian, have fupported this truth by their example, in preferring, in the latter end of their lives, the peaceful retreat of their gardens to the throne and the fceptre ; and that they found more fatisfaction in cultivating, in perfect liberty, their plants and vegetables, than in feeing themfelves crowned with laurels, or enjoying all the pomp of a day of triumph, amidft the acclamations of the Roman citizens.

EXAMPLE.

IT is a received maxim, " Live according to the laws, and not according to example." However, if we imitate good examples, we fhall never have occafion for laws to reftrain us. Good examples effectually lead us into the paths of virtue, as bad examples conduct us into thofe of vice. The wicked man fhelters himfelf in his crimes, under the idea, that he is neither the firft nor the only one who has been guilty of errors.

Good example is like a flambeau, the light of which conducts us to the right road ; but bad examples tend to countenance the wicked in their criminal purfuits. The examples of thofe who lived in former ages, teach us what will be the iffue of our conduct ; they encourage the wife to perfevere in the career of virtue, and are no lefs proper to deter the vicious from falfe courfes.

A man, whom reading has not inftructed in the different circumftances of life, is not capable of forming any project to his advantage, nor of judging what may be the iffue of his conduct ; but examples are like good fpectacles, through which we may diftinguifh at a diftance diſtance between good and evil. The general of an army, or a prime miniſter of ſtate, muſt have ſtudied the examples that have gone before them, and regulated their conduct thereby, if ever they wiſhed to obtain credit in their different profeſſions. The good examples reading furniſhes are a powerful ſpur, which make them exert every faculty to attain virtue, and ſometimes makes great men of thoſe who are as yet not far advanced in life. Happy the man, to whom a good example ſerves as a rule of his conduct, and the bad one as a warning to avoid the danger.

TRANQUILLITY.

TRUE felicity conſiſts in the tranquillity of the mind, and the health of the body. If it be eaſy to remove the diſorders of the body by the power of medicine, it is no leſs eaſy to cure the diſtempers of the mind by the aſſiſtance of reaſon. The will of God, without which no accident whatever can happen to us, ought always to be adored, and make us contented with our lot.

Reason tells us, that every agitation of the mind is useless, when the evil we suffer is without remedy. That uneasiness we feel, while the event of any thing material is hanging between hope and despair, appears more reasonable than that chagrin we feel from the weight of an actual calamity; since, in the first situation, the *perhaps* may as well turn on the bad side as on the good; whereas, in the second instance, the evil is determined, to which reason tells us we must accommodate ourselves, since impatience will not change the matter. It is incomparably better to submit with patience to the will of heaven, and to console ourselves with the hope, that as every thing is subject to change, misfortunes cannot last for ever. History furnishes us with a variety of examples of the revolutions of fortune, which sometimes raise people from the lowest pitch of misery to the most elevated situation in life,

life, and afterwards again plunged them into their former mifery and obfcurity.

WISDOM.

PHILIP of Macedon one day, being in company with feveral philofophers, afked them, what they confidered as of the moft confequence in this world. It is not at all furprifing that they were of different opinions.

One faid, that he gave the preference to water, becaufe that element occupied a greater fpace than the earth. Another infifted, that it was the fun, becaufe it gave light to the heavens, the air, and the earth. The next was of opinion, that it was the mountain Olympus, whofe fummit reached to the clouds, and, being fo high, was feen at an immenfe diftance. The fourth gave the preference to Homer, who was fo much efteemed during his life, and fo much celebrated after his death, that feven powerful nations entered into a bloody war, to *determine* which of them were actually in poffeffion of his bones.

bones. The laft fpeaker infifted, that there. was nothing in this world of fo much con-fideration as wifdom, fince it defpifes the falfe glare of things of this life, thinks little of what the world in general admire, and what the vulgar confider as the great-eft blefling.

Indeed, if we refleft on this matter properly, we fhall be brought to agree, that he, who defpifes the falfe glare of grandeur, merits more glory than he who courts or poffeffes it; and that the man, whofe virtues afford him a juft felf-appro-bation, is greater than he, to whom the rage of party may have erefted a ftatue of bronze.

Titus Livius, when he fpeaks of Marcus Curius, fays, that being one day employed in his houfe in wafhing cabbages before he put them into the pot, was waited upon by the ambaffadors of the Samnites, who came to offer him a con-fiderable fum of money, to fupport with his credit and fuffrage the requeft they had to make to the fenate. This noble Roman

Roman anfwered them very coolly: " You muft, gentlemen, offer this confiderable fum to fome other perfon, who difdains to wafh his own cabbages, and who is above being contented with fuch ordinary fare. As for me, I defire no other riches, than of having an influence over thofe who are mafters of fo much treafure."

Surely this is the charaȼter of a true hero, who knew how to derive as much glory from cleaning his cabbages in his kitchen, as from the laurels he had juftly acquired by his great exploits and famous victories. He was certainly no lefs illuftrious by his kitchen fire-fide, than invincible to the enemies of Rome, at the head of armies he commanded.

Wifdom is an ornament to the humbleft individual; but fhines with greater luftre when it is found among princes and great men, who know how to acquire it, by cultivating the acquaintance of perfons diftinguifhed for their merit and knowledge, to whom they cannot give too

free

free an accefs to their perfons. Every
prince, who is not ambitious of cultivating
wifdom, is an enemy to himfelf, and
contemptible in the eyes of all thofe who
have any difcernment, even though he
were as fortunate as Cæfar, as rich as
Crœfus, as brave as Alexander, and as
happy as Auguftus. Indeed, he would
be always unfortunate, fince, without wifdom, all the felicities of this world depend
upon chance, which are produced and de-
ftroyed according to the caprice of fortune, which equally fports with the mafter and the fervant, the king and the fubject, with the rich and the poor, and which
feems to have an abfolute power over all
the events that concern the affairs of mortals, except thofe of the wife.

YOUTH.

THERE never was feen a more
beautiful or more dangerous thing than
youth. It is the rofe of the fpring of
human life ; but it may eafily be precipitated into the abyfs of vices by in-
experience

experience and its own vivacity. It is a sea continually agitated by tempests, and full of a thousand rocks, through which we must pass in the midst of numberless dangers, before we arrive at the age of discretion.

If happiness, as some people pretend, consists in the imagination of being so, it is certainly in these times that man is the most happy, however extreme his imprudence may be, his ignorance gross, his presumption ridiculous, his judgment weak, his reasoning false, his obstinacy invincible, his comprehension dull, his passions unruly, and his foresight extremely short.

The youth thinks he knows every thing, and wishes to put theory in the place of experience; he amuses and employs himself with trifles, and readily surrenders himself into the arms of folly; indolence is his pillow, and indulgence his bed of repose; the vices pay their court to him, and the vanities accompany them; the present moment occupies all his thoughts,

and

and his cares do not extend to the future, which he confiders as uncertain; he knows not what he wifhes, for he has no fixed object in view; his refolutions are inconftant, and what he propofes has no folid foundation; fometimes he is diftractedly fond of a thing, which the next moment he as heartily defpifes; for he is not accuftomed to reflect on what he thinks or wifhes, which to him would be a punifhment. Laftly, notwithftanding what we have here obferved, happy he who paffes his youth in the ftudy of wifdom, in the application of the leffons he has received, and in the practice of virtue, as he will thereby infallibly preferve, even in old age, many of the agreeable qualities of youth.

CREDIT.

HOWEVER rich a man may be, he will not fail, if he wants credit, at fome time or other, to be as much embarraffed as he who has too much, who, not knowing how properly to manage, and take care of his credit, not only ruins himself, but involves in the same evil all those who have placed too much confidence in him. A wise man never abuses his credit, but an imprudent man soon loses it. Credit is the father of the borrower, who very often proves an unworthy son. Good faith is the mother of Credit, but she frequently brings forth children who go quite naked, who are treacherous and deceitful, and who have the cruelty to suffer their mother to be put to death when she attempts to correct them.

The prince, who loses his credit, shakes his kingdom to the very foundation. The gentleman, who fails in his credit, puts himself in the high road to ruin. The merchant, whose principal support is his credit, no sooner loses sight of it, than he becomes a bankrupt. The man, who incautiously gives credit, runs a great risk of losing his money; and he, who has a soul base enough to abuse that credit, by being generous at the expence of

P   another,

another, at laft falls into the loweft degree
of indigence, and frequently experiences
the want of the common neceffaries of life.
Avarice is generally the motive of the
lender, and imprudence and a bad confcience bring on the, latter.

I well remember, being one day at
Bruffels, that a German gentleman, an
acquaintance of mine, came to me, and
defired me to accompany him to the houfe
of a merchant, to whom he was well
known. The merchant, who was very
rich, had formerly advanced large fums
of money to my friend. On our arrival
at the merchant's houfe, we found him in
bed, to which he was confined by a
fit of the gout. He received us with
great civility, and, after we had drank
chocolate together, he liftened with
great attention to the propofal the count
made to him, which was to advance him
five hundred piftoles upon a letter of
exchange on Germany. After maturely
confidering the propofal, he replied,
" Sir, I have had the honour of feveral
times

times ferving you on your firft journeys
into this country, and it is true that you
always punctually reimburfed me the
fums with which I had accommodated
you, and I am much obliged to you
for fo doing. But permit me, Sir, to
tell you, that in thofe times I was not
much at my eafe, and I therefore eafily
ran rifks, in order to encreafe my little
fortune. Thank heaven, I have always
been fo lucky as not to lofe any thing:
but, as I have now got a fufficiency,
I wifh to be at my eafe, and preferve
what I have got without running any
chance of lofing it. So that, at prefent,
I advance no money without proper fecurity, nor truft any longer to inconftant
fortune, though I am, Sir, at the fame
time, fully perfuaded of your honour and
integrity."

Such was the conduct, which prudence
herfelf feemed to have dictated to this
old man, who, though he did not fatisfy
the demands of the count, fupplied me
with ample matter for reflection. To

fum

fum up the whole in a word; every man, who has a fufficiency to live on comfortably in his own way, and according to his condition, but ftill runs rifks to gain more, refembles the dog in Æfop's Fables, who quitted the reality for a fhadow, and loft even that he before had. He who parts with his money too freely, and lends it to the great on their own credit, refembles a candle, which confumes itfelf in the fervice of others.

MOCKERY, &c.

TO make a mockery of the infirmities of others is a vile and odious thing; it is difpleafing to God, is detefted by every honeft man, and is hated even by the impious themfelves. This diabolical inclination for mockery is the mark of a foul full of envy, prefumption, brutality, and every thing elfe the moft unworthy in a man. It is generally obferved, that he who takes delight in mockery, is generally deftitute of every quality neceffary to recommend a man in the commerce of this world.

Justice.

Mockery and raillery are nearly allied, and are equally mifchievous. The difcourfes of thofe who are fond of raillery are generally malicious, their civilities are affected, their confidence falfe, their proteftations deceitful, and their friendfhip refembles a reed, which pierces the hand of him who takes hold of it for fupport. He is beloved by nó one, but hated by all. Every one waits with impatience the moment of feeing his feet flip, that they may contribute fomething to precipitate him into the abyfs he merits.

JUSTICE.

JUSTICE is the Queen of the Virtues, and includes a great variety of bléffings it beftows on mortals. It is the fcourge of crimes, and the terror of guilt; it deftroys vice, holds folly in a bridle, protects innocence, rewards virtue, and preferves peace and tranquillity in the ftate.

The ancients, who have depicted the figure of Juftice, reprefent it with a crown

on

on its head, as the emblem of majesty, and the grandeur and glory that attends it.— They put a sceptre in its hand, to mark its absolute power, which cannot be disputed without offending heaven, and ruining the state. They put a bandage round its eyes, to insinuate the impartiality and little regard it ought to have to the appearances of persons in the course of justice: friends, enemies, rich, poor, great and little, should be all upon a level, and receive judgment according to the merit of their cause. In the left hand it holds a pair of scales, which represent its inflexible justice, which neither interest, favour, nor any other influence whatever, can in the least degree make any alteration.

Justice is frequently represented as holding a sword, instead of a sceptre, in its right-hand, and this is called the sword of justice, which is to be used in the punishments of all degrees of delinquents, whether great or little, rich or poor, weak or powerful, without the least favour or distinction.

POVERTY

POVERTY and PRIDE.

THERE is no contraſt in nature more ridiculous than that of a proud man, ſurrounded with poverty. Without hardly any ſhoes to his feet, he will take the lead in every proceſſion; and, though his linen and clothes may be much the worſe for wear, he will take his ſeat at the upper end of the table. He affects to love carelefsnefs in his dreſs, becauſe he has not wherewith to change them.— He cannot endure the ſight of laced or embroidered clothes, his ſublime genius ſoon diſcovering, that theſe are fit only to decorate ſervants, and the ſaddle-cloths of their horſes. He hates all forts of lace, is an enemy to all ornaments, and finds that a black ſtock gives to a man the appearance of a ſoldier. He wears no cloak, becauſe it is too cumberſome, and light ſhoes and ſilk ſtockings are apt to give him cold. He never powders his wig, becauſe that would make him look like a miller, and contribute to ſpoil his clothes.

clothes. He is feldom feen without a
tooth-pick in his hand, for it is very difagreeable to him to have the flesh of a
partridge or woodcock stick in his teeth.
He despifes the embarraffment of a great
train, which, according to him, is more
troublefome than proper to make a man
respected ; and, befides all thofe qualities, that are not perfonal, can form no
real merit. He is no lover of either tea
or coffee, for he fays, that it is in reality
nothing but water, and he is furprifed at
the falfe tafte of thofe who make ufe of
them. He keeps neither horfe nor car-
riage, becaufe he loves exercife, and confiders it as the fovereign preferver of health.
He never rides in a chaife, becaufe that
would be too effeminate. He never plays
at any game, becaufe he is always employed in great and important affairs,
which demand all his time and attention.
He never eats any fupper, becaufe that
would interrupt his fleep. He carries
no fmall change about him, becaufe that
would incumber his pocket; nor has he
                                    any

any fnuff-box, becaufe he wifhes to dif-
courage the practice of fnuff-taking,
confidering it as a nafty habit; though
every time he fees a box opened, he will
condefcend to thruft his fingers into it.
He fpeaks little, becaufe he does not love
contradictions, and rarely approves of
what others fay, unlefs good manners
and politenefs fometimes obliges him to
it. He never goes to operas or plays,
becaufe he does not love to be crowded,
and befides, he cannot fupport the fumes
of the candles. When he travels, he
never goes poft, but always in the ftage-
coach for the fake of agreeable company.
In fhort, his inn is at the Sun, and he
fleeps at the Moon.

While I am fpeaking of this oddity
of nature, I recollect what I have heard
fpoken of a certain girl, who accufed
herfelf to her confeffor of being very
proud. The prieft then afked her, what
he fuppofed muft be the cafe, if fhe were
rich? "No, no, father, (replied the
penitent) fo far from it, that I have
nothing

nothing in this world but the clothes on my back." " Go, go, my good girl, (faid the father) this madnefs of yours will foon leave you, and I fhall inflict no penance on you."

TO KNOW OURSELVES.

THE little knowledge a man generally has of himfelf, we may venture to fay, comes from the infatiable defire of knowing others. Being accuftomed to wander from home, where he feldom finds himfelf, he has no time to ftop to obferve what paffes within himfelf. Chilo, one of the feven wife men of Greece, bore for his motto, *Know thyfelf.* He taught others this fhort moral, which has a great extent of meaning, and is of the laft confequence; for, if we know not ourfelves, we know not in what degree we are good or bad: fo that we cannot apply ourfelves to cultivate the good, or to weaken and totally deftroy the bad we may find in ourfelves. Befides, the more we are employed in

the

the ftudy of ourfelves and our own defects, the lefs room fhall we have to complain of the difagreeable judgment the reft of the world pafs on us; and, as we do not like to hear the reproaches of the latter, we fhould be more atten- tive to the firft, the ftudy of ourfelves. We may be faid to have acquired great knowledge, when we have learned to difcover our own imperfections, and that it is a mark of wifdom to become fen- fible of our own folly, fince that know- ledge ferioufly engages us ardently to labour in the field of Reformation. Every man, whatever his fenfe and judgment may be, if he neglect the ftudy of himfelf, he will frequently commit fuch grofs errors, and will fo derange his conduct, that thofe very talents of underftanding he poffeffes, by being improperly ufed, will add to his difgrace. A celebrated author, fpeaking on this fubject, makes the following remark: " We ought at no time better to know ourfelves, than when we exert

every

every art to make ourfelves appear wife in the eyes of others ; becaufe we are generally more fond of difplaying the *little* we really know, than of learning the *great deal* we know not."

FINIS.